Dedication

*to my friend Linda who welcomed me to
Georgia and into her heart.
And to the memory of Kitty, Marie and
Kate, Maria and Louise*

Table of Contents

Chapter 1
Atlanta, Georgia, 1993

Tad Gist gazed at the reflection in his bedroom door's mirror. The tux fit okay, he decided. Now, if he could only get his stupid hair right. He didn't want to embarrass Linda in front of the Walk With Wildlife people. He spritzed his comb again and pulled it through. The curl smoothed down.

One. Two. Three seconds.

It popped up.

Maybe he should cut it off.

He fumbled through his desk drawer for scissors, grabbed a pair, and headed for the bathroom. By the time he got there, three more curls had escaped. There was no driving them back, they were slick with gel. He opened the scissor blades and faced the mirror. *If you start this,* his reflection told him, *you'll end up looking like a plucked squirrel.* Tad growled in disgust.

He stuck his head in the sink and yanked on the faucet. The sound of the water's flow muffed the first knock at his bedroom door. Another sounded, louder.

"Coming!" he called, grabbing a towel. He buffed his head quickly before opening the door to Maggie and his mother.

"Tad!" Maggie exclaimed, wide-eyed. "Is Linda getting an Academy Award?"

He grinned. "Even better, Sprite. It's an award for keeping the critters of the Chattahoochee safe. And it comes with dinner."

"Is she dressing as pretty as you?"

"Much prettier."

His mom folded her arms as she leaned on his bedroom's doorway. She was not so easy to dazzle. "Aren't you supposed to shower before you put on the penguin suit?"

The water dripped down his neck, softening the starch out of his pearl-button formal shirt. Under his mother's scrutiny, Tad felt much younger than his eighteen years. "Aw, Mom, you know—the hair," he tried, running his hand through his wet curls.

"Yeah," she said in mock sympathy. "It's tough being Adonis."

She wore her own hair tied back at the neck. It was not as abundant as Tad remembered when he was a kid, due to the hot kleig lights she worked under at Current News Network. Kelsey Doyle wasn't vain, but she was sensitive about her hair. And she was right about his. It was healthy and thick. It just had a mind of its own, like Maggie's and Dad's.

"Remember to bring Linda back here for a few moments, so we can get your photograph together before you go."

"Oh gosh, that's right. What time is it? Have the flowers been delivered? I've got to get out of here!"

Linda wouldn't care about his hair. Besides this was her night, her award. Nobody would take much notice of him. Tad snapped the towel from his shoulder, spraying Maggie. She giggled as he rushed by her.

His mother followed him downstairs. "The flowers are on the dining room table. They're lovely, Tad."

"I forgot to ask Linda the color of her dress."

"White goes with all colors. And the three camellias look perfect with the cedar twig."

"Yeah? You think so, Mom?"

"And the florist included a straight pin, in case she'd rather attach it to her dress."

Tad looked through the clear plastic case to the wrist corsage he'd chosen for Linda. The camellia meant unpretending excellence. He'd looked it up in his mother's Language of Flowers book. The flower was a good choice for Linda, he figured, as she was being honored for her work for Walk With Wildlife. The cedar was his idea too. One of Linda's summer projects was fitting a grove of cedars with bird houses. She'd absorbed the tree's scent. He liked it on her.

Tad grabbed the corsage and sped past his mother and Maggie, promising to stop back at the house with Linda. He climbed behind the wheel of his 1982 maroon Mercedes. His dad, Dr. Stan Gist, anthropology professor and part-time shade tree mechanic, had helped him polish his old car to a high wax shine that afternoon. By the time Dr. Gist had left to teach his afternoon class, the deep red Mercedes sedan didn't look its age or show its travails through its third engine and its 250,000 miles. His first car was a good choice, Tad had to admit, despite his grumbles over his parents' insistence of safety over style.

Although the fragrance of Atlanta's magnolias lingered, the coming autumn was in the air as Tad pulled into the parking lot at Linda's college dormitory. Where had the summer gone? He was just getting better at making some just-the-two-of-them time happen. Between their first courses at Morris University, Linda's work at the wildlife refuge, and his volleyball season's demands, it had not been the summer of his dreams.

Well, it was not over yet. Tad parked, then tucked the corsage box under his arm. Linda's dorm, Jackson Hall, was named after Andrew Jackson, an American President who was called the "Savior of New Orleans" for his victory over the British in the War of 1812, but who had done nothing to prevent most of Linda's ancestors from being deported West on the infamous Trail of Tears. But Linda didn't find her placement in Jackson Hall ironic. She'd laughed and said it was about time that Old Hickory did something to benefit a person of Cherokee descent.

Strolling students in casual summer clothes turned to stare at Tad's notched lapel tuxedo. He felt the drying shirt collar tighten around his neck. But that was nothing compared to the unease he felt inside. Linda's entire dorm suite had emptied. Its residents were waiting to greet him in their common sitting room. Five unofficial big sisters, eying him with brows raised and fingers tapping chins.

All in all, he preferred the adoration of little sisters.

Tad was used to Linda being surrounded by people, of course. She'd been his boss at the North Georgia archeological dig site where they'd had their rocky start back in his first high school summer here in Georgia. Then he'd been under the close scrutiny of her family and clan when he visited the Snowbird reservation on the Eastern Cherokee Nation lands.

Now she was on his turf—Atlanta. But even here Tad had to pluck her away from her dorm mates, to bring her to a banquet where she was the toast of the habitat co-sponsored by their university, Walk With Wildlife, and Garmon Chemicals. More people surrounding her. This was getting old. Would he ever have her to himself?

"Sit down, Tad," her roommate Allison urged, her polished purple nails at his shoulder. "Linda's almost ready."

"No, thanks. I'll...um, walk."

Past the low coffee table, the other four girls—Darlene, Caroline, Kelly and Renee were nodding toward the long white box and sharing secret smiles. He stopped at the floor-to-ceiling windows that overlooked the campus. He stared out as they giggled behind him. What was that all about?

Linda would explain. Here in Jackson Hall, she was in the middle of Morris University's comings and goings. Tad lived at home across town, and on the road when the volleyball team was away on its summer pre-season games.

Linda had been offered scholarships to two Ivy League schools, but had chosen Morris, here in their home state. And in his city. Well, adopted city, he was still a Buffalo, New York boy at heart. He'd never asked her, but Tad hoped that he had figured somewhere in her decision of her college choice. He felt her dorm mates 'eyes scanning him. Did they think he was a dumb jock? Linda had always met him at the door before. What was keeping her?

"Tad."

He turned. Linda was wearing a deep red dress with swirling designs woven in. Its gauzy fabric clung and played off her shape

12

so that her every movement was a dance between her and the dress. The rounded neckline left enough room to show her bone choker against her bronze-toned skin. Elaborate feather, bead, and quill earrings peaked out from her long, blunt-cut black hair. Tad felt a familiar, exciting weakness in his gut as he looked into Linda's heart-shaped face.

She was taking in his form, too. "This is very different from what we wore at the Mound Builders dig site, yes?" she asked quietly.

So, she had been thinking about their beginnings down in the mud, too. He shrugged. "Well, you look cleaner."

There. A smile. A full, rich Linda smile.

She approached the coffee table, opened the long white box that had puzzled him, and lifted a dozen long-stemmed roses from it. The scent filled the room. "They arrived just before you," she said. "Thank you."

Behind him, her dorm mates let out a collective sigh.

"I didn't send them," he said, holding out the plastic case with the suddenly inadequate, high-school-prom-like corsage. "I brought you this."

Linda placed the roses back into the box that Tad realized was from a Buckhead florist—Nico's. The heavy scent of the roses lingered as she took the plastic container from his hands.

"Tad. How beautiful."

"Who sent you those?"

"I do not know. The note was not signed. Let's leave them here."

Allison stepped forward, waving the cream-colored card. "But the note said to be sure to walk in the door of the banquet hall holding them."

"We thought you were being mysterious, Tad," Caroline chimed in.

"The note was not signed," Linda insisted again. "That was rude."

"Maybe the bouquet was from someone at Walk With Wildlife," Allison suggested.

"Or the university," Darlene tried.

Allison stepped past the other girls. "Garmon Chemicals is a British company, isn't it? I think that's your admirer. You know how the English are in all those luscious movies, with their gardens and flowers! And you're the guest of honor, aren't you, Linda?"

"It does not excuse—"

"Allison's right, Linda," Tad said quietly, though he hated to admit it. "Maybe whoever sent them forgot to sign the note, or maybe called it in to the florist and somebody there goofed. That's possible, isn't it?"

"I suppose," she conceded, frowning. "But I do not like being ordered on how to carry them. And I wish everyone to know your gift."

She brought the corsage from its case and skillfully separated one of the flowers and a sprig of cedar. She lanced them with a

14

spared straight pin and drew it through the lapel of Tad's black tux jacket. "There." She patted her creation. Her slender fingers shook, just a little. Why, Tad wondered.

"Now we are attached," she said with a shy smile. Linda was nervous, he realized now. She was a bridge person, comfortable in many worlds that were unlike her home on the reservation, so he rarely saw her that way. It made him want to protect her.

Allison presented the elegant white box into Tad's keeping as Caroline handed Linda a black velvet purse with a starburst pattern of red sequins.

"Have you got my makeup case inside?" Allison asked.

"Yes," Linda replied dutifully.

The purple outlining her already striking eyes was her roommate's idea, Tad figured, like the makeup, the lipstick, the velvet bag. Linda didn't usually wear makeup. And the only purse she ever carried was her backpack. Tad took her hand. He couldn't wait to get her out of there.

"Wait a minute, you two!"

Three flashes from cameras went off, blinding them.

"One more, one more!" they kept insisting.

"I want one with Tad!" Darlene said, claiming his arm.

"You mean Patrick Swayze here, all ready to shuffle off the tux and dirty dance?" Renee joked.

Finally, they self-timed Kelly's Olympus for group shots.

"I'm sorry Tad," Linda whispered as she draped her shoulders with the deep blue beaded and fringed shawl that Tad recognized as one her grandmother had made for her. Well, that was her own, at least. Tad liked Linda's grandmother. Delores Longknife was funny and wise.

As they stood together, Linda's head reached Tad's shoulder, as usual. Tad glanced down beyond the swirling hem of her dress to see her feet graced by high-laced, black suede moccasins. He smiled. A pair of Allison's spiked heels surely was offered.

"Nice footwear, Ahyoka," he whispered her Cherokee name.

She grinned. "Thanks."

The camera flashes finally stopped. The spots before Tad's eyes did not.

"We're in for more of the same at my house," he warned.

Dr. Gist had returned, but Tad's dad couldn't figure out who from the university might have sent Linda the roses.

"We're on a pretty tight budget," he told them. "And I can't imagine the nonprofit Walk With Wildlife being so extravagant as to shop at Nico's. I'd look to Garmon or one of the other corporate sponsors to find your secret admirer, Linda."

Once Tad's mother finished taking pictures under their dogwood tree, she placed a linen handkerchief in his breast pocket. "There," she patted it and straightened the flower Linda had pinned there, "Now you're the perfect gentleman."

"My turn!" Maggie whooped, before launching herself into Tad's arms. She hugged him hard, pressing her curly head against his heart.

"Hey, Mags," he said, laughing. "What's wrong?"

"Come home from there."

"I will. But it will be late. I'll see you when you wake up tomorrow."

"Promise?"

"Sure."

She finally released him. Then she reached into the pocket of her jeans for a folded paper. She approached Linda and offered her the colorful chalk drawing.

"Here's a dragon to protect you," she whispered. "I wrote his name, see? Uktena."

Linda stooped down beside his sister, admiring the fierce green dragon. Tad liked the way Linda always had time for Maggie. She'd giggled when Maggie asked her to twirl around to see her dress's bell-like shape unfurl. The girls he'd gone out with before Linda had barely tolerated Maggie's antics.

Tad glanced down at his sister's drawing. Uktena wore splendid horns just like the mystical Cherokee serpent. Maggie knew all Linda's stories about the beast.

Linda kissed his little sister's cheek. "A good likeness. Will we need Uktena?" she asked.

Maggie nodded.

"So, you think the banquet will be a dangerous place?"

"Yes. Beautiful, but dangerous."

Stan Gist ruffled his younger child's golden curls. "What's this? Have you been playing Tad's Escape From Demon Lair game?"

Linda folded the vibrant chalk drawing carefully and placed it in her purse.

Chapter 2

Linda reveled in the silence between them as they drove toward the corporate headquarters of Garmon Chemicals, on the grounds of the wildlife preserve. They'd had many good times riding in this old car. Tad's Mercedes was gaining in her affection, though it did not yet rival her Ford pick-up. Linda missed her clunker, but her parents needed it to carry the arts and crafts from the reservation to their shop in Cartersville. Not having any transportation except her ten-speed bike was forcing her to figure out the schedules of the trains and busses of MARTA, Atlanta's public transportation system. That was a good thing.

From the back seat, the heavy scent of roses was oppressive. She did not feel right about the gift, or the strange, commanding tone of the unsigned note. Linda wished she and Tad were going to the wildlife habitat, not the formal banquet. Perhaps after the award and her speech, the officials might lose interest in her. Then she might be able to spirit Tad away, outside.

Tad's hand left the gear shift and covered hers. "Nervous?"

"A little," she admitted. "How was your volleyball game at Valdosta?"

"All right. Valdosta's got some good spikers."

"Those are the players at the net?"

"Right."

"The ones who jam the ball down rudely."

"Linda, it's not rude. It's like stealing bases."

"Oh, I see." She was grateful for his patience and helpful analogy to the game she knew better, the one they played together at the dig site camp. She wanted to learn about this game of his, too, so that she would feel less resentful about the time it kept him away. "So the Valdosta team was good at the sneaky stuff?"

He gave out that short blast of laughter. She loved when he did that. "Yeah. But we served better, and jumped higher. I got to play three of the five games on this tour, including the decision-maker. Oh, and on the bus rides, I finished reading Deirdre of the Sorrows for our Celtic studies class."

"I am impressed." Linda smiled, wondering if he realized that he had not told her which team won that decision-maker. Was it because of the joy he took in playing? Or was he waiting for her to ask?

She wanted to ask about the cheerleader who was eying Tad as her squad shared the gym with the volleyball team's practice last week. She jumped higher, with more life when Tad looked her way. She had light hair and eyes, like his. Did she interest him?

"I photocopied our class notes for you," she said, returning to their common ground of Professor Adair's Celtic Studies class.

"Did the machine capture your spiral drawings in the margins?"

"Red Branch Cycle elements and my doodles both faithfully rendered."

"Good! Hey, speaking of drawings, it was nice of you to fuss over Maggie."

"I was not fussing. Your sister is a wise child. She speaks, I listen."

"Maybe that's why you're nervous. She was pretty serious about her dragon protecting you tonight."

"Well. I have you, too."

"Sure. You always have me." He pushed out his lapel with its flower attached. "Camellia Man."

Linda giggled. Tad could always make her feel better.

She saw the old house ahead, the one she and Dr. Milton had watched become obscured by kudzu vines as the summer wore on. The engulfed house became a journey marker for her. "Garmon Chemicals headquarters is one mile from here," she said.

Tad checked his watch. "We're not running late, then?"

"No."

Tad slowed the car and pulled over beside the abandoned house. The diesel-powered engine rumbled into silence. He

21

unbuckled his seatbelt and turned to her. "Last chance to get cold feet." he said.

She laughed. "After my roommate's make-over torture? Not likely!"

"Linda." He was suddenly serious as he touched the curve of her jaw. "You always look beautiful to me. You know that, don't you?"

Her heart swelled with feelings for this boy who looked so much more like most of the students of Morris. "Yes, I know," she whispered. "But you can tell me whenever you want to."

He grinned.

When his hand reached again for his car's steering wheel, Linda blew out her frustration. "*Uhi - so? di*," a chant in love-sick Cherokee language, came out of her too. This boy is too polite! she thought. "Tad!" she summoned. "If you do not kiss me right now, I think I might burst!"

His grin widened as he leaned across his car's stick shift. "It had better be a good one then," he said.

It was a good one. The second was even better. He tasted of peppermint and smelled of starch and camellias and cedar. Behind those scents he bore faint traces of his family— his father's sandalwood aftershave, his mother's hands, his sister's peanut butter cookie. He must have hugged them all.

"We'll be late," he murmured, when they came up for air.

"It does not matter. They will say I am on 'Indian time 'whenever we arrive," she told him, biting his lower lip playfully. She weaved her fingers through his thick, goes everywhere hair as they kissed again.

The glare of an oncoming car's headlight illuminated a stark realization. "Oh no. Tad! I have painted you."

"Painted?"

"With lipstick!"

"It will come off," he assured her, reaching for the handkerchief his mother had tucked into his pocket.

She grabbed it from his hands and began wiping his cheek. "But it is Cranberry Passion! Allison says I must wear dark lipstick because of my skin tone."

"You don't have to wear it at all," he grumbled. "Oww! Linda—"

"I am making it worse. It is so dark and you are so pale." She glanced out the window and listened for a source of water. None. Then she looked down at the smeared handkerchief. Tad backed away.

"Don't spit on it," he warned her.

"But—"

"Mom used to do that when I was a kid. Don't even think of spitting on it, Ayhoka!"

"All right, all right," she agreed, smiling that he had called her by her Cherokee name in his distress. Suddenly she realized that Allison may have armed her with a remedy among all the tubes she'd stuffed in the fancy evening bag. She rifled though them. There.

Eye makeup remover. Perhaps that would work on lipstick. She smeared the pretty rose quart tinted gel onto Tad's handkerchief as he continued to eye her suspiciously.

"What's that?" he demanded. "Let me smell it."

She lifted the handkerchief to his nose.

"All right," he conceded.

It worked. Linda enjoyed wiping away the stains almost as much as she'd enjoyed causing them. Perhaps wearing make-up was not so bad.

"What are you smiling about?" Tad demanded, as she cleared a streak from behind his ear.

"Well, I am happy that Allison provided so much of her removing magic," she explained as she swiped her lower lip with a fresh streak of Cranberry Passion. "Imagine this place later, after the banquet, when the moon is over the Kennesaw hills. Maybe we might need it again."

He leaned in close. "If we stay long enough the kudzu might wind around the car. To block our view of the moon."

"Yes. That would be nice, too."

As they pulled into the long drive, Linda watched Tad's eyes widen with interest.

"This is not like any corporate complex I've ever seen," he said, carefully observing the ten miles-per-hour speed limit once they'd entered the guarded gateway where she showed her invitation.

"Tell me what is different," she urged him.

"Well, there's no manicured, rolling lawns. No shrubs cut like sculpture. This is all meadows and woodland."

"Exactly so. And it actually saves the company money."

"How?"

"On fertilizer, turf, water and maintenance. And, Tad, the summer wildflowers, bees, and butterflies came back once the spaces were re-designed. It was so exciting!"

"And more like your home?"

"Yes. I am used to living close to the land, the animals."

"You miss it."

"Yes. But the university and Atlanta. And you, Tad. You are my home now, too."

Tad squeezed her hand. "That's good," he said quietly.

They rounded the last curve of the drive. Garmon Chemicals corporate headquarters came into view. Linda watched Tad take in the view of the low-slung complex, built in a Frank Lloyd Wright -inspired style that fit in well with its natural riverfront surroundings.

At the end of the high dock that extended out from the building, a rustic wood gazebo linked with its own reflection in the quiet waters of the Chattahoochee river. From inside, a cello, violin, and flute played a Mozart composition. Was she ready?

"Slow down, Tad," she said, realizing she was not.

"I'm only going—"

"Just a little. I was too worried about you to do a proper job fixing these layers Allison constructed on me."

She rifled through her purse as Tad shook his head. She caught him stealing looks at her as she checked her blusher and ran a comb through her boyfriend-tangled hair.

She frowned. "It is most unfair. Your curls are only more beautiful after…ruffling."

He laughed. Linda saw a tiny smear if lipstick left on his shirt's collar. Marking him hers. She liked that.

Tad pulled up under a blue awning at the buildings 'entrance. "Are you sure we're not early? he asked. "There are no other cars."

"There's an underground parking garage. Another planning decision to fit in better with the natural habitat."

"Oh. That makes sense."

As the valet reached for Tad's keys, Linda adjusted her Grandmother's shawl around her shoulders and felt its protection. She took in a deep breath.

Tad touched her hand. "The roses," he reminded her.

Linda frowned. "Sometimes your memory is too good, Camellia Man."

The strong scent snaked up between them as she lifted the flowers from their box. She thought of the kudzu place where they'd stopped, of the vines enfolding them in their beauty. She wanted to return there. Was she just nervous about her speech? She left the car, taking the flowers in her left arm, while taking the crook of Tad's arm with her right.

Chapter 3

The Garmon Chemicals lobby could have doubled as a ballroom, Tad thought.

Linda squeezed his arm. "It looks so different," she whispered.

"Isn't this where you work?"

"Well, I am used to speeding through this part on my way to the wildlife habitat."

"Hum. I'm sensing a pattern. Like we travel Atlanta streets till we get to a park?"

"Do I, Tad?"

"Hey. I'm not complaining."

They stepped down into a throng of guests in the sunken reception area. The weight of the roses in her arms seemed to be pulling Linda down. How did beauty queens do it? he wondered.

"Need to be relieved of your appendages?"

Tad turned to see the approach of a guy maybe in his fifties, with long silver hair. He took the bouquet from Linda's hold.

She smiled at him. "Thanks, Dr. Milton. This is Tad Gist. Tad, Dr. Kent Milton, of the psychology department."

Her teacher offered Tad his hand and they shook.

"You introduced Linda to the Walk With Wildlife Project," Tad remembered.

"That's right. And you're Linda's volleyball player. Paul!" he called out behind him without taking his eyes off Tad.

A guy in a formal white jacket came into view, joining them. "These are the last?" he asked in a slight French accent.

"Yes, the last." Dr. Milton said. "Paul Ferris is our maître d 'for the evening's dog and pony show," he explained, handing him the roses. "Put the flowers on the dessert table with the others, Paul."

"Others?" Linda asked. But Dr. Milton had already blended into the gathering crowd, following the man with the roses, a good-looking guy, who had grinned at the sight of Linda's dancing quill earrings.

Linda shrugged. "Well, our mystery has yet to be revealed."

Tad struggled with a sudden desire to punch the condescending smile off her boss's face when they were introduced. Get a grip, he told himself. This was Linda's night. He was here for her, not to behave like the guy expected, as a dumb, impulsive jock. Linda tucked her hand into the crook of his arm. Better.

He felt himself calming down as they chatted with other guests. He liked being linked to her as she talked about her work at the wildlife habitat.

There were advantages to having a mother in the news business. Mom had gone into Kelsey Doyle, crack reporter mode to brief him about the forty-two countries that

29

now had official ties to the city of Atlanta. Each had sent a representative to tonight's event. For years the city's government and business leaders had encouraged world-wide investment in Atlanta. The efforts made toward African countries showed. Colorful woven shawls graced many tuxedos. Beautiful Black women in golds and reds spoke with African cadences. Words flowed from languages Tad couldn't place into French, German, then English and back along translation trails to the Africans. What was that? Portuguese?

Ringing the outside of the party, a team of green fatigue uniformed men stood silently by, eyes alert. Were they bodyguards? His mother had not mentioned them in her background talk with him.

Linda was pulled toward study of international relations. As a child born of two clashing cultures herself, she was known in both the Anglo and Cherokee communities as a bridge person. It made sense that she was now expanding her bridge over the world.

As she put her hand out for another introduction, Tad heard her voice charge with enthusiasm.

"What a wonderful stone, Mrs. Garmon."

The woman looked displeased.

"Lady Garmon," the more affable man at her side explained. "Or, more precisely, Alice, Lady Garmon. And I am Geoffrey,

Lord Garmon, you see?" He turned to his wife. "None of your pique, my dear. This is America, where title protocols have not been observed for centuries. And I judge by this young lady's appearance, that class-bound titles have never been used among her own people. Am I right in assuming that you are the Wildlife Habitat's Red Indian and guiding spirit, Linda Tassel?"

"My name is Linda Tassel," Linda agreed to that much quietly.

"Also known as Ahyoka clan Waya, on her mother's side," Tad informed the couple. "That's the wolf clan."

Linda shot him a quick roll of her eyes.

Lord Garmon nodded. "Clans. How colorful. Like the Irish and the Scots. And small wonder you were attracted to my wife's 'stone 'as you call it. It is the famed Connor Emerald, reset in her necklace so that its beauty can be properly enjoyed."

Lady Garmon's French manicured fingers brushed across her neckline. Both the green satin gown and that sweep of her fingers reminded Tad of a model displaying jewelry on a TV game show. The Connor Emerald was about the size of the fist that Linda was now making in the crook of his arm. It was cut in a six-sided shape that drew the eye first, even though it was surrounded by a sparkling array of diamonds and gold filigree.

"There are wonderful stories about the stone, going back to Conn of the Hundred Battles."

Tad knew that deep voice sparked with intelligence and humor. Their Celtic Studies teacher, Maille Adair joined them. It was great to see a familiar face. A black velvet band held back her hair and matched the swirling textures of her gown.

Linda welcomed their teacher, who told great stories of Irish myth and history. "I did not know you were part of the Walk With Wildlife project, Professor Adair."

"Actually, I persuaded Dr. Milton to bring me as his guest so that I could get a look at the emerald in its latest incarnation. I'm writing about the jewel's long and embattled history."

Lord Garmon's neatly trimmed white mustache twitched. "Then you know that the Connor Emerald has been safely in English hands since the time of Queen Victoria, professor."

"Why, that's barely overnight, Lord Garmon." Professor Adair said softly, "to the Irish."

Tad sensed a crackle of tension in the air between them. Linda was quietly observing. Only Lady Garmon seemed oblivious. "Did you know I designed the setting myself?" she asked, sweeping her nails under the necklace again.

"I did not."

The two women parted from each other like repelling magnets. Lord Garmon quickly shook a nearby man's hand. "So glad you could join us tonight! You are—?"

"Richard Wunder."

"With?"

"Wildlife First. Yes. I sense you've heard of us. The not-so-nice wildlife organization. We'll fight Garmon Chemicals. In the courts, in the streets, and even at your parties. To get this river front property back to its natural state."

Linda stepped forward. "Mr. Wunder, we at Walk With Wildlife are working with Garmon Chemicals to—"

"Working with? That's the problem with you W.W.W. people! You 'work with, 'taking crumbs instead of fighting! And you, Linda Tassel. Haven't you learned anything after your people having been oppressed for generations? Do you think they will care about wildlife once they've gotten you to spout their publicity?"

He was getting too close, Tad thought. He stepped forward. A few big uniformed guys from various places around the room did the same. The closest two flanked Richard Wunder.

Lord Garmon smiled. "I should like to ask that you show your invitation, Mr. Wunder."

"You think I crashed your party? Maybe have spray paint cans here in my—"

As he reached toward his chest, white-jacketed men took a steely grip on both his arms.

"At the door, if you would be so kind," Lord Garmon insisted in a slightly tighter voice.

The two almost lifted the smaller man off his feet as they escorted him to the entrance.

"Ladies, gentlemen," their host said to the small crowd that had witnessed the encounter, his smooth and affable tone returning, "I am so sorry for this altercation. A breach in security."

Tad leaned down to Linda's ear. "Are you sure you want to go into international relations?" he asked.

"We have two years before we must choose a major?"

"Right."

"Good. I must talk with your father about the study of anthropology. The long-dead tell fine tales."

Tad marveled at how Linda went on talking with people in that gracious way of hers. He looked around at other men dressed like Paul Ferris, in short white jackets. He'd assumed they were all kitchen staff. But the bigger ones stood with their hands behind their backs and did not check the food supply or pass around trays to guests. They were private security. In addition, the camouflage wearing men, also watchful. He caught sight of many of the academics of Morris

University, who helped link the wildlife project to the community. They stood out now too. Most looked uncomfortable out of their casual tweeds. They were huddled in small groups, probably discussing the Richard Wunder confrontation.

Morris's student volunteers were easy to spot. Their formal clothes had a touch of funk—tuxes matched with high top sneakers, earrings on guys, prom dresses and costume jewelry on their dates. They were eating more than everyone else from the hors d'oeuvre table, too. Tad's stomach growled. He wanted to bring Linda over to join them, but the corporate people and international dignitaries were swarming around her.

"Overwhelmed by admirers?"

That voice. Dr. Kent Milton slid beside them. "Why don't you fetch our young speaker something to drink?" He tapped his breast pocket. "Linda," he summoned her cordially, "I have the plans for the next stage of development."

Linda's eyes sparked. "Dr. Milton! The additional acres along the river—have they been approved?"

"Come out on the dock, and I'll explain." He turned to Tad. "Take your time bringing her that drink. Aren't you athletic types always hungry? Get yourself something to eat Todd."

"Tad."

"Tad," he corrected himself with a smug smile.

Tad watched the psychology teacher steer Linda though a thicket of people and out a door. She looked over her shoulder. Tad forced himself to nod and return her smile. It hurt. He had been clenching his teeth. He didn't like that guy. He didn't like the way he looked at Linda, or touched her back. But it didn't seem to bother her. Was he a real threat? Or was it the way Tad felt dismissed? As somebody she had foolishly invited here. Someone who was way out of her league.

He headed toward the Morris students now gathered around the punch bowl, his uneasiness growing.

Chapter 4

Linda leaned over the railing of the gazebo. She breathed in the scent of the switchgrass, cardinal flowers, goldenrod and ironwood. And Dr. Milton's breath, infused with strong drink. What kind, she couldn't identify, finding mostly alcohol, with only traces of smoke and grain and pepper. He drew her shawl up to her shoulders, startling her.

"Cold?" he asked.

"No. It is a beautiful night."

"Who made your shawl?"

"My Grandmother Longknife."

"I've never seen you all made-up."

She giggled. "My roommate's concoctions. For this special occasion."

"Ah. Of course."

Linda wondered why his talk was skipping around subjects. "Where are the riverfront plans, Dr. Milton?"

"It was a good idea. It gives you a more sophisticated, grown-up look. Only the white camellias are wrong." He frowned at her wrist corsage. "A little youngish. The roses suit you better. Deep red, intoxicating. And like you—not for a boy's company."

"Boy's?"

"Your jock, wearing your lipstick on his shirt?"

"Dr. Milton—"

"I know about you, Linda. Much more than he ever will. You've been sheltered by your parents, by your mountain Cherokee community."

"Sheltered? I never thought of it as—"

"But you're a university student, free of them now. On the reservation you're everyone's pride and joy, the great red hope, aren't you? Morris has accepted you on full scholarship. Your father is a very severe man, correct? I'd bet he didn't like you leaving. And you're religious. Fundamentalist, even, am I right?"

"Dr. Milton, what are you talking about?"

"Yes, let's cut right to the heart of it, shall we? Your unnaturally prolonged virginity, Linda. That's what I'm talking about. My dear, I understand. I'm asking to be your guide. Not this boy. Your first time, with him? That would be a disaster. We—you and I, are much more complex than he will ever be. Sex between us will be adult, I promise. I think we can share something quite beautiful."

Linda felt her feet growing roots, snaking their way between the open slats of the wooden deck. "You have no plans for the riverfront habitat to show me," she said in a voice that was not hers, a faraway voice.

"My plans are for us. For your first adult experience. Don't worry, I left instructions with my little minions to keep your boyfriend busy inside. There is a powerful attraction between us, Linda. There has been since the beginning of our project."

"I never—"

"Oh, you didn't have to encourage it. The air between us has always been alive, charged. Now, as your teacher, I can guide you to the next step. Sex is powerful. Let me initiate you."

Where were her feet? Had they fanned out beneath the dock? Why could she not move? Something was moving. Her roommate's evening bag dangled against her legs, Maggie's dragon angry within.

"I am going inside now." Perhaps saying it would help her uproot.

Dr. Milton's hand grasping her shoulder felt different than other times. The times she had thought he was her friend. Everything was different now. From their work together on the grounds of the habitat she knew his strength. She'd thought him handsome, but handsome in the way her father was. She felt herself separating, becoming another Linda, drifting above this one.

"Tell me you never thought of us together?" he demanded now.

Maggie's dragon hissed. "I never thought of us in that way, no, sir."

Which of her was speaking in that flat, hollowed-out voice? She felt sorry for the

39

one caught in that man's grip. He shook her. The shawl fell to the wooden planks.

He took a long look over the contours of her body. He was yelling now, his intellectual tone disappearing. "You dressed in those shorts, those tight t-shirts that made me crazy. Of course you want this! Students throw themselves at me all the time!"

She dressed for comfort in the heat, Linda thought. But the Linda below her said nothing. Dr. Milton yanked down the corsage from her wrist. The delicate camellias fell to the deck with her shawl.

"Out here, beneath the stars, that would be appropriate, that would be appropriate, wouldn't it, Nature Girl?" His hand reached under the hem of her dress. "I wouldn't even mess your make-up, like that clumsy boy did."

The Linda hovering above them sent out a silent, desperate call to Tad. Dr. Milton pressed the shoulder of the other, the grounded girl, until she was on her knees on the shawl. The roots finally snapped, freeing her feet. But now his large hand's palm held her jaw, pressing so hard Linda felt her earring's stud tear open her neck's skin.

His grip finally eased. "Listen to the river, rough now, isn't it? Must be a storm coming. Is that how you want it? Rough, my little savage?"

Talk, the hovering one told the other, the terrified girl below. Talk.

Linda raised her eyes to his. "Dr. Milton, you could do this thing," she said quietly. "If it comes to a fight between us, you will win, because you are stronger than I am. But this is ugly. I want you to let me go back inside now. Think about how you would feel after, and let me go."

"You don't mean that!"

"I do, sir, yes."

"You never wanted me? Saw us—"

"No."

There. His hands were off her jaw, her neck. She felt a trickle of blood as she rose to her feet. The river sound rushed at her ears. Dr. Milton stood between her and the walkway, the voices, the lights of the banquet. Behind her was the rushing river. He took a step and widened his stance.

"Linda."

"Stay back."

"Don't be ridiculous. I'm not going to hurt you, silly girl. You just...disappoint me. Your shawl, here." He swept it off the deck, held it out. "Come for your shawl, Linda."

He approached. No. He was not getting near her neck again. Linda braced her hands on the gazebo's railing. A fleeting thought went through her mind. Alison had offered her spiked high heeled shoes to borrow. She wished she had. Well, the soft soled moccasins would have to do. She aimed, then kicked where Grandmother Longknife had instructed her to against a threatening man.

41

Dr. Milton doubled over with a sharp, surprised cry.

Linda turned, calling to her other, floating-above self to join her. Together, they would run faster.

Then the world around her became a blue-black blur. She was not one Linda nor the other, and had no command of the world above or below. Where was her shawl?

Light. Run for the light.

She pulled open a heavy door to see Tad, out of breath, reaching for her. When they touched, the two Lindas finally came together. Her newlyrejoined self struggled for balance as she breathed in Tad's starch and soap and hugged-by-little-sister-eating-peanut-butter scent in great gulps.

"Your flowers—" was all she could think to say as she offered him her scratched and bruising wrist. "I lost them. I lost my shawl."

"Easy. Breathe easy," he counseled, gently holding, stroking her hands.

Many people descended, surrounding them suddenly. Lady Garmon's emerald blurred, then purple spots blotted out its brilliance entirely.

"Air. She needs air," she heard Tad shout them back before he lifted her into his arms. Yes. The world was better there, Linda thought as she rested her head against his chest.

"Stay," he implored, his lips grazing her forehead. "Linda, don't faint."

"I am here, Taddeusz," she assured him with his full, beautiful name, the name that meant he was a person of courage. She tucked her bag with its wonderful, hissing Uktena against his middle. But where was her grandmother's shawl?

Intruding voices rose higher around them. She closed her eyes but felt Tad plowing through, then climbing stairs. His heartbeat quickened, but his hold on her was strong, steady. Until she heard a muffled crack, and then Tad's sharp intake of breath.

She sensed a flash of light even behind closed eyelids. Then darkness, deep darkness, like a night without stars.

Then they both fell.

Chapter 5

It was silent, at first. And the atmosphere around them had a strange beauty, in a the-world-has-come-to-an-end way. Tad was drifting on Linda's cedar scent. He wanted to move, he still felt pumped with adrenaline. He was still holding her, wasn't he? She moved. Yes, her head, still tucked in the crook of his arm.

"Linda?"

"I am here."

"Where?"

"On the floor, I think."

She was always better at directions. "The lights flashed, then went out," he realized.

"Yes."

"We fell. Down the stairs. I'm sorry, I must have slipped. You hurt?"

"No. You are the one on the bottom."

Their silent world opened up with movement around them. Shouts. People calling for a match, a phone, the police. Tad felt Linda's dress sing as she shifted. He did not want to lose her to the blur of dark movements, the rising shouts.

He found her waist. Held on as they crawled away from the voices that were making Linda's scent intensify. The effort left him winded. More than winded, he realized. Something was wrong with him. He leaned back, trying to breathe. In, out. Linda's hands traced the line of sweat that creased his brow. Her fingers found his shoulders, his arms, his—

"Aaah!"

—his ribs. Did he make that sound? Yes. The adrenaline was fading fast, pain taking its place.

"You are hurt, Tad! I crushed you when we fell down the stairs."

"No. Not you, not the fall. I think someone hit me."

"Hit you?"

"Yes. Punched. Hard."

Linda's hands went back to work. They gently unlatched his cummerbund, then pulled up his shirt. Her fingers probed. He groaned.

"Oh, Tad." She placed the heel of her hand against the pain. So cold. Her hand was icy cold. Shock. He'd been afraid she was going to faint, after she came running in from outside. Alone. Without Dr. Milton. Her eyes had been like that—blank, once before. After the snake sprang out at them in the Mound Builders 'dig site. He couldn't see her eyes now, here, in the dark.

"I'll be all right," he said, needing her closer, pulling her into his lap. "But you're not. Linda, when you were outside—"

"You heard my call. You came for me."

"Yes."

She buried her head against his chest. He only knew she was crying from the way her shoulders shook. He felt miserable, helpless.

"I must leave here, Taddeusz," she finally whispered.

"I've got you. I'll get you out, hear?"

She nodded. It was good, the crying, he knew that. People in shock don't cry. Still, it unnerved him. He didn't care who had punched him or why the lights went out. He needed to get Linda away from this place.

His eyes were now better adjusted to the darkness. And he felt cooler air rising up from a slightly opened service door. "Linda," he summoned, gently kissing her forehead. "Do you know what's down there?"

"The kitchens, wine cellar, and garage. Let's go."

They made their way to the small landing and closed the swinging door behind them.

"The stairs are iron," Linda cautioned.

Yes, he could see the swirling pattern. There must be a source of light below them, Tad thought.

"Candles," Linda said. Someone's found some—"

"Who is there?" a voice demanded.

"Paul?" Linda called down to the white-jacketed maître d'. "It's Linda. You took my roses, remember?"

"Yes, yes. You must be careful on the stairs," he said approaching, a silver candlestick in his hand. A shaking hand, Tad noticed, as they reached the last step and entered the half brick, half stone walled room.

"I was only hired for the evening, you see? I do not know where the source of power is."

"My friend Tad is hurt, Paul."

"Oh? Where?"

"His side."

Paul gave the candlestick to Linda and quickly cleared the way to Tad's injury. He did not look much older than they were. Tad hoped the guy knew what he was doing.

"Hurts like the very devil, does it?"

"Yeah," Tad admitted.

"But you can breathe okay, yes?"

"Yeah."

"Bien, good. Ice, for now. Then, a doctor for you, my friend. Wait here."

He left them in the stony darkness but returned soon with a dishcloth covered pack that smelled like shrimp and felt like relief.

Linda placed it against his side, then buttoned his vest securely over it as Paul watched. "We need to find Tad's car."

Paul brought the candle closer to Linda's tear-stained face. But he made no comment. "Allow me to help you," he offered. "We might drive out together then you may leave me by the road. To help direct the emergency crews on where to turn, yes?"

"That would be great, thank you," she agreed quickly.

Paul led them down a corridor. At the end of it, a door opened to the underground parking garage. No attendants were on duty. Paul illuminated a cork board full of hooks that held car keys. Tad found his. But Linda took them from his hand.

Yes, she was right. The pain in his side had lessened in intensity due to the ice pack and his adrenaline pumping again. Why was that? Because he felt they were running from a threat, not a power outage and a few bumps and bruises.

Paul detached the white candle from its silver holder and left the holder on the attendant's desk. He motioned them forward among the parked cars. They found Tad's old Mercedes quickly. Linda opened the front passenger side for him.

Paul sniffed before opening the back door. "German car," he said distastefully before he got in.

The headlights and Linda's skill with the stick shift got them swiftly past the exit signs to the outside. They all seemed to breathe easier there. The banquet hall was still dark, with only the sparks cast by flashlights, maybe a cigarette lighter or a candle or two illuminating the gloom.

Linda did not look back. Her foot pressed harder on the accelerator with each gear. She doubled, then tripled the fifteen miles per hour speed limit as they headed for the gates.

"Linda, take it easy," Tad tried, but her fingers gripped the wheel tighter.

They were almost out when three police cars roared across the road, blocking their exit.

Linda slammed on the brakes with a yelp. Their back seat passenger vented his anger with what Tad thought was a French curse.

Linda's hand was still on the shift when an officer's voice blared. "Cut your engine."

She obeyed.

They both turned to the back seat. The door was open. Paul Ferris was gone.

Chapter 6

Linda watched, horrified as Paul ran away from the car. Did he know how easy a target he was in that white jacket?

"Stop!" the policeman called again. "Stop or I'll shoot!"

Her mind tried to reach the young man's. Stop. Please, stop. Tad put an arm around her and shielded her eyes. But Paul finally stopped. He raised his arms above his head.

"Lancaster, you and Grey bring him in."

"Yes, sir."

The commanding officer eased back his pistol. "Keep them up," he warned. The two who took orders from him accompanied Paul back to the convergence of vehicles.

Linda felt her heart racing as he barked out more orders in the unnatural light of the cars 'beams. "Monahan, take the girl, Grey, the boy. Lancaster, you stay with our runaway."

Even as they were placed against Tad's car, his fingers stayed in contact with hers. Linda felt confused and humiliated to be searched, even though Officer Monahan's green eyes were sympathetic and her touch gentle. She hoped her fear did not show. She hoped none of them could see how much she needed Tad's support.

When they were permitted to turn around again, the officer in charge introduced himself as Sergeant Michael Sharp.

"Now, which of you was driving this car at such a breakneck speed out of here?" he demanded.

Linda heard Tad's intake of breath, so spoke up quickly, just in case he was thinking of lying to protect her. "I was, sir," she admitted. My name is Linda Tassel. I was at the banquet with my friend Tad Gist."

"And who's he?" Sergeant Sharp pointed to the captive standing between Lancaster and Grey.

"This is Paul—" Suddenly his last name was lost to her memory.

"Ferris," Paul supplied.

"Paul catered the food."

"Served, too?" Sergeant Sharp asked the surly man in white.

"Supervised the servers," Paul corrected.

"Paul helped Tad, who is hurt. He helped us get to the car after the lights went out, you see. You are here because the lights went out at the banquet?" Linda's curiosity surfaced despite their predicament. Why had two cars and four members of the police force been sent to a power failure, even one at the Garmon Chemicals headquarters?

"I'm the one currently in charge of questioning, Miss Tassel," Sharp reminded her.

"Of course," she murmured, tucking her head against Tad's arm. She hoped her eyes were not still swollen. Officer Monahan was giving her a knowing look.

Tad took up her cause. "What Linda's saying is that we were looking for help. Because of the power failure, we fell down a stairway, you see—"

"Are you hurt?" Officer Monahan asked Linda, kindness added to the suspicion in her voice, Linda thought.

"Not me. Tad is. Here," she explained, lifting Tad's vest and shirt to reveal the makeshift ice pack.

The young policeman who'd padded them down shrugged awkwardly. "The kid did feel lumpy. And smelled fishy," he reported.

The policewoman lifted the dishtowel. "Swelling, bruised," she reported back. "Can't tell if there's any fractures, sir," she reported.

"Do you think you require immediate medical attention, son?" Sergeant Sharp asked.

Linda hoped Tad didn't feel the panic spiraling out of her at the thought of being separated from him. She hoped he would speak the truth, for his own sake.

"No, sir."

He was not turning red. Tad's light skin colored in the rare times that he lied. He was telling the truth, then. "Linda was concerned about me, and getting help. She's really a great, within-the-speed-limit driver, normally, Sergeant. And Paul, he said he was going to flag emergency vehicles down."

"So why did he run?"

Tad felt the same way Linda did, she was sure— grateful to the maître d 'for his help, and unwilling to betray him after his kindness. But why did Paul run?

Sergeant Sharp turned. "Are you in the habit of fleeing the help you were going to flag down, Mr. Ferris? Then ignoring police demands to halt?"

"I have a right to not answer your questions," he said.

The policeman's brow raised. "Are you a citizen of this country?"

"My family has been here for three hundred years. I do not have to spit out a green card for you."

Something was happening to Paul's accent, Linda realized. So did the police sergeant, who smiled.

"Thought if I got your dander up that fancy French would turn gumbo, boy. We've chased down a few members of your illustrious family. You have gone by a different name, I think? In Louisiana?"

Stony silence was his reply.

"Search the car," Sergeant Sharp commanded his officers. "Thoroughly."

The flashlight beams began probing. Why? Linda saw a silent apology from Paul's eyes before they led him to a squad car.

Sergeant Sharp turned to them. "Now, if you two would lead us to your fancy party at a sensible speed, Miss Tassel, we'll see if we can get some lights on and some questions answered."

Once back in Tad's car, he growled. "I guess that was supposed to be an apology."

Linda gripped the wheel hard. "I guess."

"Don't worry about me, Ahyoka," he said, using her sacred name.

"You need help. What are they looking for? Why take only Paul into their custody?"

"Why did he run? Everybody's got questions."

"I want this to be a dream. I want to wake up, not go back there, Tad."

"Linda, what happened?"

She blinked away tears. "Not now," she whispered, hoping it would be enough.

It was. He leaned over kissed below the wound in her neck. She felt his lips against the dry blood. And the deep rumble of his anger. He loved her. What would he do, if she told him? What could she even tell him, of the two Lindas, one above and below? What had happened? It was even now blurring and lost to her.

She turned the wheel to get around the last bend. The lights were back on at Garmon Headquarters.

When they stepped inside, the police officers behind them, Linda's nightmare notched up. The guests were now disheveled, their clothing torn, their carefully designed faces smudged, their hair astray. They reminded Linda of the snarling wildcats of her mountains.

Lady Garmon advanced on Linda ahead of all of them. "There she is!" she shouted. "That Red Indian girl stole my necklace!"

Chapter 7

"Of course it was she," Lady Garmon insisted, as her husband tried to calm her. "Everyone saw how she looked at my emerald! Why else did she run away?"

"We were not running away," Tad said as evenly as he could.

"Don't," Paul Ferris warned, now beside him. "Say nothing until you talk with your lawyer."

"Lawyer?" Tad felt himself coloring as he realized he'd shouted the room silent. "Listen, Lady Garmon," he tried, "the lights went out on everyone. Linda and I, we fell—"

"Not before she grabbed my necklace!"

Lord Garmon stepped forward. "Alice, you already told me you couldn't see who—"

"It had to be her! Roses! I distinctly remember the scent of roses! And she carried in a whole bouquet of them, as if she thought herself the Queen of the May, instead of some charity student."

That was enough to make Paul Ferris break his stony silence. "And I took them from her hands, Madame, to set them on the dessert table. So I carry the scent as well, no?"

Tad smiled. "Oh, and I took them from the car."

"Write that down, a harried Sergeant Sharp told Officer Grey.

Professor Adair stepped forward, her gown torn at the sleeve and a smudge on her cheek. "You know, officers, I admired the flowers too. Closely."

"Your name, Ma'am?"

"Adair. Maille Adair."

"Got that?" Sergeant Sharp asked his assistant.

The young police officer scribbled furiously. A low murmur began among the Walk With Wildlife people. "I touched them when they were on the table," one volunteered.

"So did I," another said.

Tad leaned close. "We're having an 'I am Spartacus 'moment, I think," he whispered at Linda's ear.

"Spartacus?"

"You know, the old movie with Kirk Douglas and... never mind," he said, remembering that the Snowbird Reservation probably didn't have a movie theater, and Linda grew up without a TV. "Let's just say you've got friends." He kissed her forehead.

"Actually, I plucked one." That voice's English accent stood out. "For my buttonhole, Father dear."

"Neil, this is not funny." Lord Garmon warned a man who looked like the guy they

57

now had playing James Bond, Timothy Dalton.

Neil Garmon's mouth quirked up, a real Bond move. "Small wonder you had me removed from the board of Garmon Enterprises, I cannot be trusted to leave table decorations in their place, eh?"

He approached Lady Garmon with a weaving step. "Smell, Alice," he invited, offering his hands under her quivering chin. "You're quite right, a strong scent. Distinctive, are they not, these roses?" He turned to Sergeant Sharp. "I'm afraid my stepmother's keen sense of smell has given you a roomful of suspects, Detective," he pronounced.

Sergeant Sharp looked exasperated. "I'm not a detective! We called some in—I wish I could freeze the lot of you till they get here. Now don't anybody touch anything, y'hear?"

He looked down at the pad where his fellow policeman was still writing. "I can't make out but every other word of this gibberish, Grey! Where's Monahan?"

"After you told her to call the detective division, you said she should help Lancaster find the guest who's still missing, sir."

"Oh, yeah. Should have sent you looking instead. She can spell." He looked over the rose-scented line of people forming in front of the policeman. "Listen, folks, you could have your I.D.'s ready. And those of you hurt? We've got the best E.M.T.s in the

58

country coming soon, and you can, oh, get out of the line to be treated." He looked above their heads at two officers approaching from outside. "Monahan, Lancaster, there you are! What have you got?"

Tad watched Monahan's eyes zero in on Linda as Lancaster spoke, "Doesn't look good for the missing guest, a professor, sir."

"What?"

"We may have more than a robbery here, Sergeant, Monahan began.

"Signs of a struggle," Lancaster continued. "A broken railing over the river. We might need a diving crew for a body search."

Tad felt Linda shrink against his side, as all the eyes of the room focused on her."

"I did not mean to hurt him," she said.

Lady Garmon began screaming. Sergeant Sharp barked orders to his officers and the guests. Officer Grey scribbled. Paul Ferris looked from Tad to Linda, shook his head, and tapped his finger against his lips.

Tad touched the small of Linda's back. "I'm here," he said. "I won't leave you."

Though she neither responded nor looked up at him, he felt her tension ease through that place in her back. He briefly lost himself in the power of it. Look alert, another part of him warned. Her world was turning ugly. She knows only beauty. She's lost. And she did as much for you, when you were lost in her mountains.

He looked up when he heard the commotion at the doors. The five men who came through them wore suits, but Tad knew from Sergeant Sharp's sigh of relief, that they were the men he was waiting for, the detective unit.

One more person, a short man with bowed legs trailed in behind them. He was dressed as if he'd spent the day fishing in the Chattahoochee. His blue pork pie hat fit askew, its well-crafted lures dangling. His sharp eyes belied his casual appearance as they scanned the crowd before him. Tad knew who W. C. Hawes was looking for, so he didn't even try to hide. He remembered the police chief's shark-like smile when he'd once told Tad what the W. C. stood for: We Convict.

The eyes stopped their search. "Well, you two," he drawled. "Appears you're up to your eyeballs in trouble again."

Chapter 8

Linda kept breathing in Tad's scent through the weave of his jacket, because people who smelled of metal were all around them. Guns.

"Ahyoka," Tad summoned her gently. "Look. It's Chief Hawes."

Linda finally raised her head. She remembered the small, wiry man of about sixty years. She remembered his hat, full of bright feathers and shiny beads, to call the fish to his hook. She smiled in spite of herself, in spite of the terrible trouble eating her soul.

"Good evening, sir," she said. "Visiting town?"

He took her hand as if he were a guest at the banquet, not sequestered with them in this small office off the banquet's floor. His grasp held. "That's right. Visiting friends in the area. Fishing this part of the Chattahoochee is the best it's been since I can remember. Got you Cherokee folks fighting us to clean up your sacred land and waterways to thank for that."

"It pleases me that you have benefitted."

"Now, I heard my Atlanta colleagues running a check with the National Crime Information Center on you two. Thought I'd come over and provide a personal reference."

"We appreciate that, sir," Tad said, She was still trying to understand what Chief Hawes had said. What was wrong with her? "Don't we, Linda?" Tad prompted.

"Yes, of course."

The man finally released her hand. "You're as cold as ice, youngster."

"You do not see us in our best light, sir. And Tad is packed in it."

"Packed in—?"

"Ice. He is hurt. Please, look."

"Aww, Linda," Tad growled, as Chief Hawes inspected Tad's injury, and whistled. "Being a college boy hasn't made you any faster at dodging trouble, has it?"

"No, sir."

"Have the E.M.T.'s had a look at that?"

"It can wait."

"No," Linda whispered through her fear. "You should go now, Tad."

"I'm not leaving you."

"Chief Hawes is here in this quiet place with me now."

"Chief in Cartersville, Linda," their friend reminded her. "I'm retired from the Atlanta police force, remember? Not that I still don't pull a little weight, mind. Listen, Tad. You two are in my personal custody. Linda can rest here with me until you get back. She's right, son. Let them check those ribs, make you more comfortable. We'll be waiting. Right here."

"You sure?" Tad asked her.

Why had she not seen the pain on his face, through his body, more clearly? "Yes."

"All right, then." He leaned over as she rose to her toes to meet his kiss. He cupped the side of her face. "Kv: ke: yu: ?" he whispered the Cherokee phrase before he limped out of the room, toward the flashing lights of the emergency vehicles.

The lights blurred. Linda felt her tears flowing. She thought she would be all right without him beside her, but she was not. And she could not stop, no matter how hard she pressed her fingers against her mouth. But she was not alone. She felt Chief Hawes's khaki vest with many pockets drop over her shoulders, smelling like fish, like Tad did, once Paul Ferris packed him in ice. It warmed her, the vest, but freed even more tears.

"That's right, that's good," the policeman soothed, easing her down on a cool leather couch. He called to the woman stationed outside the room to bring a blanket.

Once within its folds, Linda felt safe enough to cocoon herself, clearing her mind of all thought, filling it with images of the colors of her shawl when she danced. She remade herself into a butterfly, one from her favorite meadow of the Snowbird reservation, the one who had kept them company that spring day when Tad kissed her, over and over, his lips like feathers.

He'd said that phase then too. It meant that he loved her.

There was a man and a woman in the room with her now, speaking in low tones. She closed her eyes in order to stay in the meadow, with Tad and his butterfly kisses. But she heard them.

"Any change on the missing?"

"No, sir."

"Listen. I don't know this Paul Ferris," Chief Hawes said. "Maybe he was up to no good. But I do know these kids, Monahan. The boy's hurt. Couldn't they have been going for help, like they said?"

"They appeared to be running away, sir," the woman answered. "And I work a lot with domestic violence, rape cases, Chief. I see signs in her that I've seen before."

"Like?"

"Scattered speech, movements. Shock. Beyond physical trauma. The kind of shock when someone you know and trusted does something unthinkable. And fear. A woman's fear, sir. That she won't be believed."

There was a long silence.

Then Chief Hawes spoke though the green colors behind Linda's eyelids. "Detective Windgate thinks we ought to get statements from the kids separately. What do you think?"

"I don't agree, sir. Not in this instance."

"Why?"

"Look at her. She needs him."

It took great courage for the woman to say these things, Linda sensed, to this man who knew an older time, a time when battered women were told to be better at cleaning their houses, better cooks, better lovers. She must prove a worthy beneficiary of this woman's courage, Linda decided.

"Would you stay in the room with us, Monahan?"

"Me, sir?"

"Don't tell anyone, but I'm too fond of these kids to be entirely objective."

"I'd be glad to stay, sir."

"And they will want notes on the conversation."

"Sir?"

"Got a pencil? I hear you can spell."

Linda heard the woman laugh. "Well enough, sir."

The butterflies finally rested the frantic beating of their wings. Tad enfolded her in his arms. The sun went down on the meadow. Linda felt safe enough to sleep.

When she opened her eyes again, Tad was beside her, looking better.

"Water?" he offered her a fancy crystal glass from the Garmon event, which now seemed a million years ago.

She nodded, sitting up, cupping her hands around his as he brought the glass to her lips. The blanket slipped off her shoulders. "Where is my shawl?" she asked Tad.

He looked up at Chief Hawes, then at Officer Monahan standing beside him. Her police hat was off, and Linda saw her blond hair braided around her head.

"Where is my shawl?" she asked again.

"Being held. Evidence," the policewoman said gently.

Linda nodded, taking Tad's hand, remembering not to lean on him.

"It's all right," he said, bringing her closer. "I'm all taped, like a regular mummy."

"And, your ribs?"

"Cracked," Chief Hawes supplied his answer with a punctuating grunt. "Three of them. I don't know how he was standing."

"Oh, Tad."

"It's not so bad. Hairline fractures, the E.M.T. thinks." Tad's eyes were very bright. "They've got X-ray stuff right in their truck, Linda. It was cool. Paul Ferris was right, to ask about my breathing, remember? And to pack me in ice. There's no damage to my lungs, or breathing. Just the muscles."

"Those will feel much worse," Chief Hawes informed him, "once that shot they gave you wears off."

Was that why Tad's eyes shined so, Linda wondered, and why he talked a little faster than usual?

"It's a good thing the nature of your injury backs up your claim, Tad. You were hit. Hard."

"And that's good?"

Linda giggled into Tad's shoulder.

"Buck up, you two," Officer Monahan warned, looking up from her note pad, "this is supposed to be an interrogation."

"And you're in luck that the two of us are getting your statements," Chief Hawes seconded. "Poor Detective Windgate has got his hands full with what's becoming a crisis of international proportions out there." He gestured toward the door. "Two hundred people from eighteen countries. A crime scene that lost electric power, two guests among the missing."

"Two?" Tad asked.

"Yes. Dr. Milton, and a Richard Wunder, leader of an animal rights group that sometimes goes beyond civil disobedience to make its point, if I recall."

Officer Monahan gave a soft, impressed whistle as she leafed through her previous notes. "That's right, Chief."

Linda remembered Chief Hawes's good memory. He never jotted down a thing. Did he ask Officer Monahan to as an excuse to assist him in other ways?

"I understand Mr. Wunder was asked to leave earlier in the evening after a confrontation with you two. That right?"

"We saw him ... encouraged toward the door before the lights went out," Tad offered.

"Well, Windgate's crew are checking the grounds for him. He was willing to have us have a crack at interrogating you, as you fit the profile of likely jewel thief suspects, too."

"How's that, sir?" Tad asked.

"You were both in Lady Garmon's proximity when the lights went out. And she's got the whole case solved for us: swears Linda had eyes for the stone, and pointed it out to her accomplice, Tad here. Now, why wasn't it found on you or in your car after your escape attempt? That's due to another accomplice—"

"Paul Ferris?"

"Kindly refrain from interrupting the aristocratic detective work of Lady Garmon, you transplanted Yankee carpetbagger. Lady Garmon even says your iron-fisted assaulter was another of your gang and performed his duty for looks only."

"He could have cracked one rib for looks," Tad groused.

"In this scenario," Chief Hawes continued, "you three were about to meet Iron Fist, who is in possession of the necklace, at your pre-arranged hide-out. We should have let you drive off and 'given chase 'to find out where that is, of course. See? We all made mistakes. A colorful hypothesis, ain't it?"

"Why would we do such a thing?" Linda asked.

"Ah, motive. We have plenty of choices, according to Lady G. She's not sure which fits best. Does Professor Adair—oh, did I mention she's part of your gang, too? Does she have you cast in her spell of Irish retribution for the loss of the Connor

Emerald? Or is Tad the pawn in Linda's scheme to ransom the emerald to get the remaining riverfront land approved for wildlife habitat?"

Linda shook her head in dismay. "I didn't make a very good first impression with Lady Garmon, did I?"

All three of her companions laughed at her observation, which puzzled her at first. Then she decided that it didn't matter. The sound of it cut through the ugly web of suspicion like spring rain.

"Yes, Lady G, that crack countrywoman of Agatha Christie, is way ahead of me on this investigation," Chief Hawes confided. "Now, before you two are smashing rocks at Leavenworth prison, I'd better collect your side of the story of what went on here tonight. I hope you remember my opinion of eyewitness testimony. I wouldn't hang a mad dog on the grounds of it."

Officer Monahan shot Chief Hawes a look, of what? Warning? But Linda smiled at her new friend, trying to assure the policewoman that she trusted the man in the funny hat to believe her.

Chapter 9

Tad had a hard time controlling his temper as he listened to Linda answering questions. Was his anger amped up by what the emergency medics had put in his veins? He felt charged, wired. Fight it, he told himself. Stay calm. Linda needed him calm. He took her hand as she began.

"Dr. Milton said he had the river front plans, while we were still inside," she explained softly.

"Do you remember that, Tad?" Chief Hawes asked.

"Sure. He sent me to get Linda a drink while they went out. Told me to eat. Made a remark about athletes always being hungry. Then this girl kept asking me about my last game." Stop with the details, Tad told himself. He was running off at the mouth because of the buzzing inside him.

Chief Hawes 'eyebrows disappeared in the rim of his hat. "You didn't have a great first impression of Dr. Milton, I take it?"

"No, sir."

"What about you, Linda. You knew him longer?"

"Since the wildlife project was launched in July. We worked together, first on the planning committee, then on the birdhouses in the cedars. He drove me here, then back to my dormitory on volunteer days, Tuesdays and Thursdays. He took a few of us to Mitchell's in Underground Atlanta for lunch once."

"Did you enjoy his company?" Officer Monahan asked.

"Yes. I respected him, and the work we did together. I respected Dr. Milton as an elder."

She sounded so lost. Tad began tracing a small circle in her palm. For her, or to ease his own helpless anger?

"Did you talk about personal things?" Monahan probed further.

"A little." Tad heard the pain notch up in her voice. "I told him that I grew up on the Snowbird reservation. That we then moved to Cartersville when Aunt Theda needed to be near her MS therapy center. He asked me once if I was seeing anyone, and I told him about Tad. But mostly we talked about the project, and about the university."

"Okay, thank you," Chief Hawes said. "Now let's go back to the scene. You're at the gazebo with Dr. Milton. Take it from there."

Linda stared at the gap between her two police questioners. Tad closed his fingers over hers. Her trembling rode up his arm. Calm, stay calm, he reminded himself.

"I asked to see the plans," Linda explained quietly. "The ones for the riverfront property. But he kept talking about how I looked, my shawl and make-up.

And about Tad, and about my father being harsh and severe."

"What?" came out of Tad before he knew it. "Your father is the coolest—"

Officer Monahan shut him down with a look.

Linda's cheek brushed Tad's shoulder before she spoke. "It was as if Dr. Milton was remaking me into another person, someone he would like me to be. The talk confused me and I said so. 'What are you talking about? ' I said. Yes, I remember saying that before..."

"Before what, Linda?" The sharp-eyed woman pressed.

"Before the time becomes cloudy."

"Think" the policewoman urged. "What was Dr. Milton talking about?"

Linda took in a shuddering breath. "Sex."

Tad felt a low growl forming at the back of his throat. Chief Hawes 'look muzzled him this time.

Monahan continued. "He asked you to have sex?"

"No. Not asked. Told. Told me it is what I wanted. Remaking me, you see?"

"It's not what you wanted."

"I was frightened by his words, and by his hold on me when I said no."

"How did you say no, Linda? What words did you use?"

"I do not remember."

Linda looked at Tad. Why hadn't he been faster reaching her? Why were all those people in between them?

"I tried to get away," Linda whispered.

"Where did he hold you?"

"My shoulder, I think. Then, here." She lifted her wrist, The scratches and swelling where her corsage had been. Tad felt like jumping out of his skin at the sight. "And, I think—" She touched behind her ear. The policewoman leaned forward, gently lifted Linda's hair back from her face. She winced. "Take a look, sir," she advised her superior officer. Chief Hawes leaned forward.

Tad felt a twitch beside his eye as he saw the trickle of dried blood, the ugly purple bruise on Linda's neck. He was losing it. He needed to punch something, even the wall, like some dumb jock.

He felt Chief Hawes hand on his shoulder. "Breathe," he said. "She's all right now."

Officer Monahan sighed. "We know this is hard for you, Linda," she said. "Please tell us what happened then."

Tad felt the squeeze of Linda's hand. Cold, again. "This is a sickness that has come over him, I thought," she said. "I tried to talk it away."

"What did you say?"

"I don't remember exactly. I wanted so badly to be away, you see? So part of me was. Away. I said that he would win, if we fought.

That this was not what I wanted, something like that. Why can I not remember?"

Linda leaned against him. Why didn't they leave her alone? Tad slipped his arm around her waist and they all waited for her to continue.

She sat higher. "He let me go, then. I thought, maybe this is over. But he had my shawl. He held it and blocked my way past him. His words, they taunted me. I only wanted to be away; I did not want to hurt him!"

"What did you do?"

"I kicked him."

"Where?"

"In his groin."

"And?"

"I ran. I don't remember anything after that. Not until I saw Tad jump to reach me." A flicker of a smile crossed her face. "It was a fine jump."

Chief Hawes leaned forward. "Think, Linda. Did you hear anything behind you? Splintering wood? A splash?"

"No. I—" She shook her head. "No."

"How close was Milton to the railing?"

"He? No. I was against the railing. Leaning back on it to get more power, there in my feet."

Chief Hawes 'eyebrows rose. "And you kicked straight out?"

She nodded. Her hair shifted and Tad saw the injury on her neck again. Why didn't they stop? Why didn't they leave her alone?

"I only wanted to bring him down," she said. "So that he could not come after me. Is that what happened? Did he come after me? Fall into the river? Did I push him? Why do I not remember?"

"We're still at the information gathering stage," Chief Hawes said gently. "You remember that stage, don't you Tad?"

He unlocked his jaw. "Yes, sir."

"What were you doing while Linda was outside?"

"I went to the buffet table. Talked with some of the student volunteers. But not for long. I wasn't comfortable."

"How so?"

"Nothing seemed right. I mean, I was trying to be polite, give Linda a chance to go over the riverfront plans, but... Are you writing all this down?" he asked Monahan suddenly, loud enough that she dropped her pencil. He ran his hand though his hair. "I sound like a stupid kid."

"Relax, Tad," she urged, picking up her pencil.

"Go on," Chief Hawes said.

"I grabbed a couple of bottles of mineral water. To hell with being polite, I decided, I don't like that guy, I'm going to find Linda. I looked out toward where they'd gone, but there were so many doors facing the river. I headed for the closest one, but Lady Garmon was standing in front of it, talking to a guy with a woven shawl at the shoulder.

Monahan flipped though her notebook. "General Tenatu, from Liberia," she supplied the name.

"Go ahead, Tad."

"As I got closer these big guys, four of them, dressed the same only without medals, blocked my path. They started yelling at me. But I had to get past them because I saw Linda come though the doorway. So I handed them the bottles of water, and...well, I jumped over a table."

"How did Linda look to you, Tad?"

"Out of breath. She couldn't talk. People crowded around us. I was afraid she might faint, so I picked her up, tried to get her away. That's when everything went dark."

"Do you remember that part, Linda?" Monahan asked.

"Yes, I remember pulling up my purse, well, my roommate's purse, before the darkness."

"That bag?" Monahan pointed to the bejewel purse in Linda's lap.

"Yes. I raised it here, against Tad's—"

"Ribs," Chief Hawes finished for her.

"May we see the bag?" Officer Monahan asked.

Linda handed it to her.

Officer Monahan removed Tad's lipstick-streaked handkerchief first. Next came Maggie's dragon drawing. The sight of it made Tad remember. Protection. The dragon was Linda's protection, Maggie said.

Wow. There was no way he'd be telling the police that detail.

The policewoman drew out Linda's makeup case and unzipped it. She peered inside. "Looks like you'll have to go shopping."

"None of this is mine! Oh, Tad, look."

Tad glanced over her shoulder. The containers of whatever-girls-carry around in those small bags were broken. Glass shards were swimming around inside the plastic case.

"Yes. I remember now," Linda said quietly. "The sound of breaking, then Tad pulling in his breath."

"What does this mean?" Tad asked their questioners.

Chief Hawes exchanged grim glances with the policewoman. "You got hit by a professional, Tad. Linda's bag might have saved you from much worse damage."

Chapter 10

Over the next rise in the road the lights of the Atlanta skyline appeared. The city looked beautiful, like her childhood picture book images of the city of Oz. Linda glanced over at Tad. She had reclined the front passenger seat as far as it would go to keep him more comfortable on the way home. Tad's eyes were closed, not in sleep, but in pain, she was sure. Linda didn't want him in that darkness alone.

"Tad?"

"Yeah?"

"It is hard to believe they let us go."

"I know what you mean. This isn't the end of the evening we had planned, but we could be in jail."

"We have a debt to Chief Hawes, I think."

"Detective. He told us to call him Detective Hawes in Atlanta, remember?"

"Right. Detective."

"Tad, do you—" She bit her lip.

"What, love?"

"Do you think Dr. Milton is dead?"

"I hope not."

She nodded.

"Because I want to kill him."

Linda couldn't pretend to be shocked or even disappointed. Because she felt only pride in his fierce devotion.

She turned off the Peachtree Road exit as he spoke again. "How did your parents sound on the phone?"

"Worried, but better when they learned I was with you and have your family's protection tonight. What about yours?"

"The same. Mom will want to poke around my bandage, then send me to our family doctor tomorrow, so I guess your chauffeur duties aren't over yet."

"Good. I like driving your car. Maybe your father will find one for me some day."

"I'm sure he can. He's got a sixth sense for finding little old ladies who are finished with their ancient Mercedes sedans." He reached over and covered her hand where it rested on the knob of the stick shift. The cool feel of it helped her feel safe, like the evening breeze through the pines of her home.

"My parents are glad you agreed to stay with us, Linda. They would be uneasy without you close."

"Taddeusz. This is like a terrible dream."

"I know. But we're in it together."

The front porch light shone at Tad's house in the Atlanta neighborhood of Inman Park. Linda loved the old trees and greenery planted among the bungalow houses that were built long ago. She smiled when she saw his parents walk out from the shadow of a dogwood tree.

Kelsey Doyle was still in the linen suit she often wore on the air during her job at the Current News Network. The suit was a little wrinkled and her coral lipstick smeared. She and her husband had been kissing there, under the dogwood tree. Tad's parents were like hers, she thought—the physical part of their love for each other deepened and made their troubles lighter over their years together.

That was all Linda had been surrounded by, that kind of love, based in respect and friendship, before tonight. Before the twisted words and actions of a man she had trusted. The thought of Dr. Milton made her wrist and neck ache, made her well up in confusion and sorrow. Linda remembered her plans to spirit Tad off tonight, under the fine moon and the kudzu. If those plans had worked out, her lipstick would be smeared, too. And she would not feel as she did now— that she needed a mountain of burning sage to help her feel whole again.

His father helped Tad from the car. She hoped the medication he'd been given before they left would help him sleep. He looked so tired.

His mother stood outside the driver's door, waiting for her to rise out of the car. Kelsey Doyle kissed her cheek and draped a soft cotton sweater over her shoulders as she emerged. "Tad told us the police had your shawl. I hope this will do."

"Thank you," Linda whispered, battling back tears.

"We're glad you're both home."

When she had first learned of Tad's mother's profession, Linda wondered if it was possible to stay human while investigating corruption, accidents, deliberate violence. She'd learned differently. Linda felt overwhelmed by Kelsey's compassion and generosity.

She did not even ask questions as she led Linda to the guest room. Fresh flowers blossomed from a vase on the dresser, a soft cotton nightgown was laid out on a wicker chair.

After she'd showered for too long and was ready for bed, there came a soft knock on the room's door. She opened it to Tad in his corduroy robe.

"You look terrible. Go to bed."

He smiled, as if she'd said something much nicer. The middle finger of his right hand touched her forehead, then traced a path to her chin. "If you need me—"

"You will know." She rolled her eyes. "You always know. Spook."

"You didn't call me that in front of Chief 'We Convict' Hawes. Or tell about Maggie's dragon standing guard in your purse."

"Or about splitting myself in half."

"What? How?"

"On the dock. I had to pull out of myself. That is why I don't remember so well, so exactly as the police wanted. I was not all the way inside myself."

He looked away, his glance strafing the floorboards.

"I had to, Tad. I was so afraid."

He nodded, but did not look at her. Why could he not speak? Was he angry?

"Should I have told that part?"

He shook his head.

"I said enough, then?"

"Yes."

"Tad, Linda!" They heard his mother's loud whisper from his parents 'bedroom. "Get some sleep!"

Tad looked at her at last. No, he was not angry or ashamed of her and her visions. His eyes held suffering, even as his humor produced a mock frown in his parents ' direction. "Good night, Ahyoka."

His fingers grazed her cheek as he kissed her softly. His lips left hers with a small pull of promise. And reverence for her shattered self.

But the memory of his kiss could not keep her safe when the dreams came, making her sweat and flinch. She forgot where she was, who she was, in the dreams. She felt blinded by a nameless, formless terror, reaching for her from under the river's depths. She bolted up, clutching the blankets.

Tad sprinted into the room, with only a gasp, holding his right side from the effort, reminding her that the night had taken a toll on him, too. He stood by the bed, fatigue shadowing his eyes.

"Move over," he whispered.

She did. He climbed in beneath the covers, filling in the terror's space.

"Tad, your parents—"

"Told us to sleep," he finished her objection. "This is the only way either of us will."

He was a practical boy, a wonderful boy, Linda thought, as she burrowed into the space he opened beneath his arm. His deep brown robe felt as soft as she had imagined. Nestled securely, she lay her arm across his chest, anchoring her hand inside the robe, over his heart. She was asleep by her third intake of breath.

"Linda?"

She lifted her head, opened her eyes towards the sound of the child's worried voice. The uncertain light of pre-dawn heightened Maggie Gist's blond curls as she stood at the bedside.

"Tad's gone," the worried little voice whispered.

"No. He's here, beside me."

"Why?"

"I had bad dreams."

Maggie nodded. "Sometimes he hears me first, before Mama even, when I have bad dreams. Can I cozy up with you, too?" she asked, while launching herself.

"Yes, but—"

"Oww!"

"...he is hurt," Linda finished as the little girl tumbled in between them.

Tad blinked as he raised himself to his elbows. "Maggie. Where's Linda? What time is it?"

"I am here," Linda whispered, reaching over his sister's head, her fingers easing the lines of worry from his brow.

"You can bug-doze some more," Maggie promised. "It's still dark time." Her small hand patted down his chest until he sank into the mattress again.

"Oh, okay, Sprite."

Linda kissed the little girl's cheek. Tad's nickname for his sister fitted her perfectly. She was his small but fierce, protecting *yûñwi tsunsdi'*.

"Tad?" she called her brother softly now.

"Hmmm?"

"I should have made a dragon for you too."

"I'll be all right, Maggs. Your dragon protected us both."

Chapter 11

Doctor Fine scribbled out a prescription. But Tad had already decided to dutifully stuff the paper into his jeans 'pocket and make do with aspirin. It was bad enough his cracked ribs wouldn't allow him to drive. He wasn't going to dull his mind and reflexes on a prescription pain reliever. Not while the evidence mounted against Linda. Even now, he was itching to get back to her where she sat in his family doctor's waiting room.

He liked Dr. Fine. He was about Tad's parents 'age, maybe late forties. Tad had never seen him in a tie or white lab coat. He wore casual clothes in crazy color combinations to amuse sick kids. Copies of Modern Maturity mixed happily with Highlights for Children, Newsweek, Sassy, Cricket, and National Parks magazines, testament to his appeal across generations. Dr. Fine even made house calls.

Linda had sensed his matter-of-fact goodness, too. Enough to let go of Tad's hand and let the doctor look at her injuries and talk over the night before.

Now Dr. Fine shuffled through the papers on his big roll top desk until he found a sheet of his office stationery. He began writing a letter to Tad's coach. That he couldn't stuff in his pocket and ignore.

Tad tried to think of anything but the letter, even how tight the new bandages felt against his injury, to mask his reaction to the glide of the doctor's pen and its peacock blue ink. If he could hide his disappointment from Dr. Fine, maybe he'd have a chance of hiding it from Linda. She didn't need another burden.

Don't think about what the letter meant to his hopes of making the varsity team, he told himself. Focus on getting information.

"Might the guy have survived, Doc?"

Dr. Fine leaned back in his swivel chair. Its wheels caught on one of his toddler son's stuffed animals—a grey squirrel. He picked it up and tossed it on his desk before he answered. "How far was the fall off the dock?"

"Eight, maybe ten feet."

"Good swimmer?"

"I don't know. Wait, yes, I do." Tad remembered. "Linda talked about them swimming at a picnic the habitat had for volunteers. Yeah, he can swim in river currents."

"There were signs of force, of injury?"

"Broken railing. And blood on Linda's shawl."

"Whose?"

"Both. His, mostly, Chief Hawes said." Tad felt his throat tightening. Not about the man whose body might be floating down the

Chattahoochee, but about the blood behind Linda's ear, and the scratches at her wrists.

"And there's been no word from or sign of Dr. Milton so far today?"

"No, sir. Not before we phoned Chief—I mean Detective Hawes this morning."

"Doesn't sound good."

"Yeah, I was afraid of that. What about the possibility of Linda remembering better? About after she kicked him? And how the blood got on her shawl?"

"You're out of my field now, Tad."

"Come on, Doc. You treat us as whole people, don't you? And Linda's practically family."

"I've noticed the resemblance," Dr. Fine said with a wry smile as he removed his gold wire rimmed glasses. He wiped the lenses on the tail of today's anti-fashion statement, a palm tree strewn Hawaiian shirt. "Okay, look. It sounds to me that Linda did what she had to do last night, Tad." He eased back in his creaking chair. "Fight, flight. They are basic human responses and Linda is a strong and healthy young woman. She's got some bruises, scratches, a small cut on her neck. They are all healing nicely.

"Now, what else she had to battle—her professor's mind games, his betrayal of her trust, that was mixed in with the assault. That will leave the most lasting scars, I imagine."

"Like, nightmares?"

"Nightmares, jangled nerves, memory gaps. They are all normal parts of recovery. Not great for police investigations. But normal." He took a deep breath. "Tad, Linda's trust, her devotion to you—"

"That's not normal?"

"No, it's not." He smiled, twirling the dented squirrel's tail. "It's extraordinary. You know that, don't you?"

"Yes, sir. And it's not one-sided."

"Good. Now get out of here. Can't you see I have an emergency operation to perform on this critter before Christopher wakes up from his nap?"

They found Linda on her hands and knees in the waiting room, stacking multi-colored blocks into a neat wall in the children's play corner. She was only a year younger than Tad, but there on the floor, swallowed inside one of his mom's light blue sweatsuits, she looked younger, more fragile than he'd ever seen her.

Dr. Fine squatted down, pulling a lollipop from his shirt pocket. Linda took it, smiling.

"*Wa-to*, Doctor. Thank you."

"It was good meeting you, Linda." He looked up at Tad. "Good luck with this character over the next few days."

"He cares for others better than himself."

"Exactly. You," he nodded toward Tad, "Flat out bedrest, two hours, minimum.

Midday, each day, until I see you again on Wednesday."

"Yes, sir," Tad mumbled, hoping he wouldn't mention—

"And get that prescription filled."

—the prescription.

Tad touched Linda's shoulder. "We can go now."

"To the Morris Gymnasium," the doctor reminded him. "Deliver that note. Now."

"I will, sir," Ted promised. "Thanks for everything, Doc."

"Stop crushing the envelope. I already have a reputation for being too loosey goosey."

"Oh. Sorry."

"To whom are we delivering your doctor's note?" Linda asked as she slid behind the wheel.

"Coach Nelson."

"Your volleyball team. Of course. How long before you're able to play?"

Tad tried looking out the window. It didn't work.

Linda's voice became small and sorrowful. "The season is over for you?"

"Yeah."

"Oh, Tad. That is terrible."

"No. It isn't. I was falling behind in my coursework, not just on the reading for our Celtic Studies class. And the guys gave me a hard time about writing papers on the bus, about, wanting better grades than a C average."

She let him go on, making excuses for why what was terrible wasn't, really. Inman Park, then downtown Atlanta and all its Peachtree streets sped by. He didn't stop talking until she stopped the car in front of Morris University's gym. When he finally turned from the window, he looked down. Linda's hand lightly covered his fisted one. Tears shone in her eyes.

"I am so sorry, Taddeusz," she said.

"Linda, don't."

"Don't what?"

"Be so nice to me. Dr. Fine is right. I'm a terrible patient. I'll only get worse."

"I can bear it."

He touched her cheek. "You want to come in?"

"Yes."

Even pushing the heavy Mercedes door open was a strain. How did he even wonder if he could pick up any of the volleyball season? Well, he had an immediate need now. To find some aspirin.

Linda's eyes were shaded with her concern. He couldn't hide much from her. But she was the one with the nightmares, with the deeper scars. The sooner he gave his coach the doctor's letter, the better. He took her offered hand. She walked close to his damaged left side and half a step ahead all the way to the office. She was protecting him, he realized.

He missed her warmth once he left her in Mrs. Shaeffer's company and entered Coach Nelson's inner sanctum.

After reading the letter, the short, compact man whose hair was always slicked back like he'd just hit the showers raised his head, frowning deeply. "Didn't think a dinner party for tree huggers would be so dangerous, or I would have advised against it."

Tad tried to shrug. Even that hurt.

"What went on out there last night?"

"I'm pretty confused about it myself, sir."

"Brass?"

"Sir?"

"Did it fell like brass? You know, like metal when you took that punch to your gut, brass knuckles?"

"I never got hit like that before, Coach."

"I don't like the looks of you. Running a fever?"

"No, sir."

"Did the EMT give you a shot?"

"Yes."

"What are you on now?"

"I..." Tad hedged.

"Your doctor wrote you a prescription, didn't he?"

"Yeah. Yeah, sure he did."

Coach Nelson growled, shoved open a drawer, then thew a green bottle his way.

Tad caught it, letting out a small yelp of surprise.

"Nothing," Coach Nelson determined for himself.

"Sir?"

"Stop playing the dumb jock, Gist. "You're not on any pain meds—your reflexes are too good. Why?"

"Tad studied the cracks in the linoleum floor. "I need my wits about me, sir."

"I see."

Coach Nelson went to the room's water cooler, poured Tad a paper cup full, handed it to him, and pointed to the green bottle. "Take two. Now. It's just over the counter, but extra strength. Have you got someone to take you home?"

Tad nodded and swallowed down the capsules with the water.

"Where is he?"

"Visiting with Mrs. Shaeffer. Only, it's not—"

"Where? Coach Nelson demanded again, looking past his glass door to where Linda was chatting with his secretary.

"My friend's not a he, sir," Tad explained.

"That little girl? She's going to help you get around?"

Tad smiled. "Linda's stronger than she looks, Coach."

Coach Nelson walked back to his desk. "We'll miss you on the team," he admitted as if it were a state secret. "You were promising,

Gist. Don't usually take first year students if they're not on athletic scholarships. Keep your average up. Try out again next year."

"Yes, sir. Thanks." He tried to return the green bottle but the coach held up his hand. And finally granted Tad one of his toothy smiles. "Keep it. Every four hours. And, Tad?"

"Sir?"

"How about considering, when you're feeling better, I mean, coming in to help me train the team I've got left?"

"I don't know that I could, sir."

"You've got a good head on your shoulders, Gist. Good with people, too. Even tempered, even when the guys weren't easy on you with your bus studying. You earned their respect. I think you could be a help to me with this bunch."

"Thanks, Coach."

"Part time. Once a week. Will you think about it?"

"Yeah, sure."

Coach Nelson pulled open his desk's top drawer. He took out a shining silver stopwatch on a black cord. He put it around Tad's neck. "Here. To help you think it over. And to make sure I see you back here in person with your answer." The coach looked out his doorway to the reception area beyond. "And, Tad?"

"Sir?"

"You and that little girl. Look after each other, y'hear?"

As he left the office, Tad saw that both Linda and Coach Nelson's secretary, Mrs. Shaeffer had moved down the hallway. They were silhouetted in shadow as they talked over the healing properties of the aloe plant hanging at a window. He smiled. Linda was using her Bridge Person skills to establish a common bond with the green-loving Mrs. Shaeffer.

Linda belonged everywhere.

Tad shoved the stopwatch inside his shirt. The capsules he'd swallowed in Coach Nelson's office were starting to work at masking his pain. Until he felt a hard slap at his shoulder.

Chapter 12

Linda winced, recognizing two of Tad's teammates. She stopped mid-sentence and tore down the corridor.

"Hey, Gist, where did you hide Dr. Milton's body?"

"Never mind the body, where's the emerald?"

They didn't know that their blows to his back were hurting him, Linda thought. It eased her fury only a fraction.

"Get back!"

Both were over a foot taller than she, and the red-haired one was so wide he blocked out the window's light.

But he had the grace to step back. "Hey, listen, we heard he was taped up but—"

"No, you listen. Do not touch him again!"

She hoped it was the fierceness of her look that backed them up further, but they were looking over her head, behind her. She turned to see Coach Nelson staring them down from the doorway.

His plant-loving secretary joined Linda. "Have you some business here?" she asked the boys.

"No, ma'am."

"Just passing, Mrs. S."

"Keep moving," she instructed.

They did.

Tad grinned at the secretary, who Linda realized was even shorter than her own five feet and three inches. "So. You're the power behind Coach, Mrs. S." he said.

"Never mind that," she answered, her grey curls bobbing with her head. "You look awful. Get in here. Sit down. Have a brownie." She opened a tin on her desk.

Linda could tell that the sweet-faced woman wanted to feel useful. And her brownies were delicious. She sat across from them, watching Tad. She liked watching him too, the way he took big, appreciative bites of food.

Mrs. Shaeffer sat back. "I'll be glad when Dr. Milton shows up and the police find who caused all that havoc, so we can get back to educating you two."

"Do you think Dr. Milton is alive?" Linda asked quietly.

"I couldn't say for certain, of course. But he likes being the center of attention, that one. I wouldn't be surprised if he makes a late appearance to garner a few more headlines for himself."

"Why?" Linda asked.

Mrs. Shaeffer leaned closer. "I'm a friend of Margery Atwood, his secretary. Margery and I, we've seen teachers come and go here at Morris. Dr. Milton is one of the high-profile ones. Probably wowed them in his interview. And he's always getting published in the journals and getting his name mentioned in local papers for his community projects.

"Now Margery and I, we live in this city. And we're part of the university community too. All his famous charm aside, Dr. Milton's habit is to stay on a local project a semester or two, then he moves on, leaving committees scrambling. And his socializing wore his poor wife out with hosting parties for celebrities, rich alumni donors and such, that's what Margery says."

"Dr. Milton is married?"

"Not any more. Not the commitment type. We all saw that, except his poor wife, of course. Well, Mrs. Milton is Mrs. Greene now. Dr. Greene works in the biology department. Less flamboyant but of a more sterling character."

Linda nodded, feeling that Mrs. Shaeffer was much wiser about Dr. Milton than she had been.

The hallway began to fill with students. Some pointed at Tad and Linda. Linda had been taught that pointing was rude. White people did it often, so she was sure it was not the same for them. But it was hard to endure.

"Well, the ten o'clock classes are ending," Mrs. Shaeffer said cheerfully. But her glare kept the other students moving.

Linda scanned her watch. She was still not used to everything having a time space at the university. "Tad," she summoned his attention away from his enjoyment of his second brownie, "our Celtic Studies class begins soon."

Tad swallowed. "Oh, yeah."

"It's good that you are jumping back into your lives here," Mrs. Shaeffer approved. "Let the police do their job. But don't be a stranger here at the sports complex, Tad. Laps in the pool will do wonders to strengthen your muscles once your doctor gives his okay. Linda and I can talk plants. And baseball season will be here before you know it. I hear nothing gets by you at shortstop."

"Where did you hear that?" he asked, eying Linda.

"I protect my sources. Now, don't let anyone know I fed you brownies before lunch. Bent my own rule, you two looked so pitiful."

Once outside, Tad took Linda's hand. "You told Mrs. S. about my baseball position?"

"I had to let her know I was worthy of your affection, yes?"

"Worthy? I think you're now in her will."

Their Celtic Studies classroom was empty, with a hastily written cancellation note on the door.

"Until further notice."

Linda recognized Professor Adair's sweeping handwriting. "We must find out about this," she said.

He nodded and they set off for the offices of the English Department.

It was a beautiful, crisp fall day, and many of the campus's oak and ash trees were turning glorious hues. Linda tried to concentrate on the variations of yellows, oranges, but that became impossible. Wherever they walked, she heard whispered conversations stop abruptly, replaced by false-face smiles, and more pointing.

The doors of the English teachers' offices spun off a large, open middle space that contained desks of assistants, whirring copy machines, phones, faxes, and computers.

They found Professor Adair's corner office door and knocked.

"Until further notice means until further notice!" came the shout.

Linda turned the doorknob and walked into the tiny, windowless, book-lined space ahead of Tad, wanting to shield him from another assault, even of words.

Professor Adair was on her hands and knees, reaching under a bookshelf, three cardboard boxes around her. She was dressed in jeans and a grey sweatshirt emblazoned with the words "We should all be feminists."

Her frown softened when she saw them. "Linda, Tad. My partners in crime. Come in, come in." She held up the scrappy paperback book she'd discovered under the nearest shelf. "I've been looking for this forever. To cite in my thesis. I'll have plenty of time to complete it now."

"Have you been fired, Professor Adair?" Tad asked.

"Suspended. Also, 'until further notice.' Until they find the Connor Emerald in my flour bin, I suspect. Then they'll fire me. Leave the door open, Linda," she instructed, more loudly. "Wouldn't want anyone thinking that this is a secret meeting with my two young collaborators."

The heads in the common work area turned their attention back to tasks at hand.

Professor Adair pushed a stray strand of red hair behind her headband. "Clear a chair and sit. How are you both?"

"Tad's ribs are cracked. Three of them," Linda said.

"Heard that, but I was hoping they'd got it as wrong as everything else. And you, Linda. How are you?"

Their teacher seemed to look inside her. She felt Tad's hand cover hers before he spoke. "Why did they suspend you, Professor Adair?"

"Listen," she said, her voice sounding a little more like the engaged teacher most of her students admired. "We're all a little twitchy in our under-the-microscope position after last night's events, aren't we?"

Linda nodded slowly.

"I'm gathering my thesis notes and research and heading home. I'd advise you to do the same."

Exactly the opposite advise from that Mrs. Shaeffer had given them moments ago. "Why?" Linda asked.

"Because the university community is a fishbowl. Because maybe none of us are safe."

"Wait, slow down, Professor Adair," Tad said. "Who are 'us?'"

She gave them both a green-eyed stare before she sighed. "You're babies. But bright babies, so, why not? Close the door," she commanded.

Linda obeyed. Professor Adair sat at her computer, scanned the screen, then pressed a print command. A series of eight sheets soon sailed out of her printer.

She handed them to Linda. "Here you go. Put it in your backpack, for reference."

"What is that?" Tad asked.

"A list of everyone who attended the banquet. I grabbed it off inter-office. I knew Dr. Milton would have some overworked graduate student feed the information in for him, so I copied it early this morning. Look at the names. We can't count on the police."

"Why not?"

"We are not dealing with amateurs, my dears. We have been set-up. Framed. We'll need to get ourselves out of this. Before they come for us."

"Professor Adair—" Tad protested.

"I'm Irish-American, with a few cousins in County Mayo. Does that make me a gun-toting terrorist?"

"No. Of course not."

"But that's where the police will be directed. And to my mother's birth name."

"Which is?"

"Connor."

"Yes. They will reduce us all to blood-thirsty tribal savages. You know a little about that game I imagine, Linda?"

"I do," Linda said quietly, thinking about Lord Garmon calling her a red Indian.

"Do you know which foreign country's nationals own the most American real estate?" Professor Adair asked them.

"No," they answered together.

"Guess."

"Japan? Saudi Arabia?" Tad tried.

"No. Great Britain. And their propaganda network can't be beat, not even by Israel's. Great at painting themselves as the noble good guys, our staunch stiff upper lip allies. Even though there are millions of Americans of Irish descent, thanks to British propaganda, the Irish become bloody terrorists—that's their power over hearts and minds."

"But I do not understand what this has to do with a stolen emerald," Linda said.

"Of course you don't. I'm babbling. I babble when I'm nervous. I'm sorry you got entangled in this. It was foolish to ask Kent Milton for an invitation to the event. I thought we were becoming colleagues, that it was so long ago."

"What was so long go?" Tad asked.

"We, Dr. Milton and I were...involved. When I was an undergraduate. I fell for that old 'my wife doesn't understand me 'line. It was messy, awful. I didn't have the confidence, belief in myself that you have, Linda. I'm making excuses. I was wrong, I was sorry, I tried to get out of it—let him think it was his idea that we split up, even. I should have stayed completely clear of him when I took the teaching job, but I thought he'd changed. And with all this community service and devotion to causes. I thought that I could ask this favor, as a colleague. But men don't change."

"Change?" Linda asked.

Professor Adair shook her head. "I wanted to see it, that's all. It's been hidden away in a vault my whole life. I've been writing my thesis on its history for the past three years. And I have a right to my anger at it being in English hands, and now so vapidly used as the centerpiece of a gaudy ornament by that woman! I only wanted to see it, you understand?"

"No," Linda admitted.

Professor Adair found an index card and pencil. "Here's my address. The police are not even asking the right questions."

"What are the right questions?" Tad asked quietly.

"Come over to my place, say, seven tonight? Let's figure out how to help each other."

Chapter 13

Linda frowned. "If you will not get that prescription filled, you need to eat."

"I had the brownies."

"Real food."

What was the use of trying to hide anything from Linda, Tad wondered. And maybe she was right, and that eating would help him feel better. He hated the ache in his side, and how tired he felt. It made this confusing morning even harder to take.

At least they were off campus, and away from Professor Adair's rapid-fire speculations. And all those curious stares. Tad rested his head against the trunk of a dogwood tree in a sheltered part of Piedmont Park. It was one of Linda's favorite patches of green in the city.

"Lie back," she demanded as she removed the backpack from her shoulders. "It is midday, remember? Time for flat out, feet up, rest." She shoved the backpack under his feet. "Two hours."

Tad grunted. "I forgot about your phonographic memory."

She laughed. "My what?"

"Well, some have a photographic memory, but you remember everything you hear."

"Only important things. Like doctor's orders."

"He said 'bed rest. 'How are you getting around that?"

"There are spring flower beds planted here, under the dogwoods."

"That's a stretch."

"Yes," she admitted biting her lower lip in that way that made his heart flip. "Should I bring you home, Tad?"

"No, no! Two and a half out of three isn't bad!"

"Good. Stay put. I will be right back."

"Where are you going?"

"There is a food stand around the corner. I am buying you lunch, Camellia Man."

Tad grinned. You know this park better than I do, and Maggie's dragged me through half a dozen times."

"Ah. Always using the dragon topiary entrance?"

"Exactly."

"Rest, Tad," she told him again.

Tad watched Linda walk away, looking almost like herself, in spite of his mother's oversized sweatsuit rolled up at her ankles and wrists. Here in the larger world of Atlanta, they didn't feel the stares that their unwelcome celebrity status had gained them on campus. Tad closed his eyes, just for a few seconds, he thought. He felt Linda's fingers sweep lightly across his brow.

"Did you forget something?" he asked.

"I have gone and come back."

"Really?"

"Really. Here is proof." She opened a brown bag beneath his nose. "Smell."

Pastrami on toast. Warm and loaded with sauerkraut. Just the way he liked it.

She removed their waxed paper wrapped sandwiches and drinks from the bag. Tad was surprised to see two bottles of Coke. Linda was more health-conscious than he was. She favored juices or mineral water.

She frowned at his amused reaction. "Atlanta," she complained, "the only city in the world where you can get a sandwich as exotic as yours, but all that's available to drink is Coca-cola ®!"

"This is its hallowed birthplace." He tried to sweep his arm over the park's landscape, but stopped short when pain intruded. He hoped Linda didn't notice.

"As if I could forget!" She laughed, but her eyes were concerned. "Do you have medicine?"

"Coach gave me some."

"Is it time to take it?"

Tad didn't try to hide, or look away. He felt suddenly overcome with gratitude for this girl sitting beside him. He took her hand.

"I love you, Ahyoka."

Gruff, low, a whisper. But he needed to tell her again how he felt. Especially since all she went through, before he'd reached her last night. He picked up her hand and kissed into her palm.

"I was going to give you my coleslaw portion anyway," she said softly, her eyes blinking.

"You don't have to. Just don't cry."

"I am not crying!"

"Good. Eat."

"You eat." She unscrewed his Coke bottle. "But take your medicine first."

"All right." He popped two capsules into his mouth and washed them down with the Coke.

She watched him suspiciously.

"I'm not going anywhere."

"Correct. Not for two hours," she said, tapping her watch face.

The sandwich tasted great out there in the open air. Tad tried not to wolf it down. He knew as soon as he finished, Linda would want him flat on his back again for the midday rest Dr. Fine had insisted on. He began to feel better, much better. Pain reliever and food helped, he was sure, but the warm autumn day and Linda's company contributed too. He took the last bite and chewed slowly. Maybe he could convince her to—

"No." Her lips formed a straight, firm line.

"I didn't say anything!"

"Lie still."

"Aw, Linda, it's bad for digestion to—"

"I once read that you can digest while standing on your head," she said sweetly. "Isn't the human body amazing?"

"You want me to stand on my head?"

He didn't know anyone else who looked so beautiful while frowning. "I want you to rest your pastrami-filled self as Dr. Fine said."

"But I feel better."

"Do you want to stay that way?"

"Just a short walk down Peachtree," he tried. "To that pastry shop you like?"

Her eyes widened. "Shall I have Chief Hawes handcuff you to that dogwood trunk when he joins us?"

"Detective Hawes is coming here?"

"Yes. I called him from a pay phone at the lunch stand. He has been following up on something I told him last night. And he plans to bring—"

"Of course! I should have known that you two would stray off the beaten path."

And, as if conjured, W.C. Hawes appeared, then climbed up the rise to their dogwood. He still wore vacation fishing clothes, though he'd removed the lures from his hat. When Tad tried to prop himself up higher, a cold paper sack landed softly on his chest.

"Down, boy," Detective Hawes said in a deadly earnest vice.

Tad sighed. "I know when I'm outnumbered."

"And out classed."

Detective Hawes and Linda exchanged satisfied looks before she relieved Tad's chest of the cold package. "And as you were trying to bribe yourself out of your rest time with our love of sweets," Linda informed him, "look. Detective Hawes has brought dessert."

Caught, red-faced.

"Your mama's right, son, you are a weather vane," Hawes observed, sitting beside them on the grass, "wouldn't need any fancy lie detectors if everyone was so transparent."

"I hope you've come to tell us who stole Lady Garmon's necklace, sir."

"Hmmn. You have not divested me of the notion that Yankees are as demanding as they are impatient, boy. Eat your ice cream before you're wearing it."

Linda hid her giggle behind her hand. Tad rolled to his good side and plunged into his treat—a hot fudge sundae, featuring what he always ordered at Mitchell's, chocolate chip ice cream. Linda opened her own favorite, a "Broadway," chocolate soda with coffee ice cream.

Linda smiled. "Our chief listens well. And I did not even have to tell him where Mitchell's was."

"Aww, I've been going to Mitchell's since before you were gleams in your parents' eyes," Hawes said, digging into his peach ice cream and fruit salad sundae. Tad would never in a million years remind him that his choice was a Mitchell's specialty called a "Sweet Sixteen."

"Auburn Avenue was my first walking beat as a patrolman," Detective Hawes continued. That's where Al Mitchell's was, before his grandson moved the place to its chichi location in Underground Atlanta."

"But the Underground Atlanta Mitchell's is its original location, sir," Linda said.

"What?"

She nodded. "Al's ancestor Constantine set up shop back when it was a railroad depot in the 1800s. It was above ground Atlanta then."

"Well...well, it's a blasted shopping mall now! Oh, why do I try to match wits with college-educated archeologists?"

"We are also prime suspects in your current case," Linda reminded him. "Can you tell us how it is progressing?"

Detective Hawes balanced a chunk of pineapple on the end of his spoon. "Let's get something straight, youngsters. I'm not part of the Atlanta police department anymore. I'm not officially on this case. I have earned some privileges, that's all. And you two ought to be in school."

"All done," Tad informed him.

"We had only one class today, Detective Hawes," Linda elaborated, "and it was cancelled."

The policeman made a sour face. "College! And I hear you won't have any more volleyball games to keep you out of trouble this semester."

"That's right, sir."

"Well, I'm looking forward to heading back to the Dahlonega hills where the timber rattlers cause me a lot less worry."

Tad looked away. He wished he felt like serving some come-backs to Chief Hawes ' humor about his lost volleyball season, but he wasn't ready.

He felt a hand on his shoulder. "Could be worse, son."

Tad smiled slowly. "Yeah, we might be charged with stealing the Connor Emerald."

"And murder," Linda reminded him.

"Well, Tad's got an alibi for that one."

"Based on eyewitness testimony," Tad reminded him. "You know how unreliable that is. You wouldn't hang a mad dog on it, you said so yourself. And speaking of mad, how is Lady Garmon this morning? Accusing anyone else?"

"No one's gotten near her. Under sedation, doctor's orders. The Garmons are not the most co-operative of crime victims. But rumor has it that Lord Garmon has hired multiple private investigators to find that fortune in gemstones. And to keep their findings quiet. Especially since his son's got debts."

"Neil Garmon?"

"That's the one. If he's got sticky fingers, the whole investigation might implode."

"What about your missing guest? Richard Wunder?"

"The Wildlife First guy? He turned up. With a hangover and no alibi. We're keeping an eye on him. But there are many entities stretched pretty thin on this case."

"How is that, sir?" Linda asked.

"The Atlanta police department is told it's on touchy ground, revolving around the U.S. involvement in these new peace negotiations in Northern Ireland. And there's that international guest list from last night already telling us that. We've got six translators at work just getting statements. It will be another day before all two hundred people are deposed. I was glad to get out of that tower of Babble downtown, believe me!"

"Any interesting information at the ice cream parlor, sir?" Linda asked.

"At Mitchell's?" Tad asked.

Detective Hawes smiled. "Based on a tip from that wise little lady beside you, I learned that besides being a regular, Dr. Milton did more than bring small groups of students there during lunch hours. He was a late-night customer too. Loved the 1950s atmosphere, reminded him of his youth with the jukebox full of Chuck Berry and early Elvis tunes."

Tad saw Linda stroke her arms against a chill that was not in the air of this warm day. She noticed, gave him a fleeting smile, then rested her hand on his shoulder.

"Seems he brought a few ladies on his late-night visits," W.C. Hawes continued, "And Gus Mitchell thought they might have visited other, more hard liquor establishments first. The latest was a redhead whose flashy fifties clothes Gus remembered. But not her voice. She never spoke, he said."

"Not a word?" Tad asked.

"That's how Gus remembers. That and the hair. What do you call the style? Big hair? Popular among the youth of our first daughter when she was a teen. If any of this connects, I'll be very glad you remembered the professor's hang-out, Linda."

"No trace of Dr. Milton's been found yet?" she asked.

"Afraid not. The Chatahoochee's a funny river. If he's dead, it might take a while to recover the body. But he's got plenty of reasons to lay low for now."

"He does?"

"You could press assault charges."

"If I could remember better. And if people believed me."

Detective Hawes swept off his hat and scratched his head. "What happened to you...well, Monahan's awfully good at helping women feel safe talking. From what she's found on campus, she thinks your teacher is more than a ladies 'man. We're getting a profile. Wouldn't want any of my daughters within three hundred yards of the guy. He might be in real trouble. If the Chattahoochee hasn't gotten him first, of course. He's got reasons to lay low. But so do you, slugger."

Tad frowned. "More like 'slugged.'"

"Any new faces come back to you when you woke up this morning? A guy with a gleam of steel wrapped around his knuckles, maybe?"

"I'm afraid not, sir."

"What about Paul Ferris?" Linda asked the detective, "Are you still holding him?"

"We are."

"Why?"

"We're not finished questioning him."

"How many questions do you need to ask?"

Hawes held up his hand. "Paul Ferris has another name, which he volunteered before our check on him went through. He's also Paul Ferradeau, born into and bred by a family of New Orleans jewel thieves."

Chapter 14

Tad bolted up, before Linda gently eased his shoulders back to a reclining position. "Detective Hawes, you are supposed to be helping me," she complained.

"Sorry. Downtown, they jumped at the news, too. Most think they have their man, what with his flight from the scene. Some thought they had enough to charge him."

"You did not."

"Well, no. First off, the guy's been clean since his first incarceration finished three years ago. I mean squeaky clean. Not a visit to his parole officer missed, not a traffic ticket."

"But he changed his name."

"Yes, legally. For business purposes, he said. But a French name can only help in food catering, I would think. Like that fancier French accent he puts on over his N'Awlins drawl for his customers. Maybe he's trying to distance himself from his family. Father, brother and uncle, they all have records stemming from the family trade. They even boast they have family ties to Jean Lafitte and his pirates."

"That's why the name change and the move to Atlanta?"

"He put himself through a fancy cooking school here. That man wants out of the family business, I'd wager my next trout expedition on it."

"So, why did he run?" Tad asked.

"I suspect he knew we'd find out that he convinced his boss to low-bid enough to get the job. Along with himself as maître d'. He was working for free."

"So he could get a look at the Connor Emerald?"

"It's legendary in history, and among jewel thieves. It's still in his blood. Paul Ferradeau cut his teeth on stolen diamonds and precious gems. Was Paul Ferris going to content himself with a look? Or could he not resist the pull of generations?"

Linda smiled. "Why Chief, you sound like a poet."

The small man shrugged. "Too much meditation time while fishing, I suppose. And I'm not—oh, I give up."

"Sir," Tad asked, "Do you think Paul stole the necklace?"

"I don't know, son. But I don't think Paul Ferris is dangerous. Even when he was a thief, he never carried a weapon, or resorted to violence. Another point of family honor among the Ferradeaus. So, if he did steal it, I'd rather have him out leading us to the necklace than in jail. Now, if you'll finish your rest period in peace, Tad, I've got some social obligations to fulfill. I'm supposed to be on vacation."

"We appreciate the update, sir," Linda thanked him. "And the ice cream."

"My kids only got a custom order from Mitchell's when their report cards came in. So work hard this semester, you two, and earn it." He handed them both a card with his Atlanta position crossed out, his Cartersville address and phone number penciled in, and his vacation address and number scrawled on the back.

"When are you going to spring for new business cards, Chief?" Tad asked.

"When you two start staying out of trouble."

Linda consulted her watch. "Now we have some things to talk about to keep you down and resting."

"Some things? Like Paul Ferris going back to his former profession?"

"Paul did not do it, Tad. He only wanted to look at the Connor Emerald, just as Professor Adair did."

"Linda. The man's a thief. A convicted felon."

"Was a thief," she corrected. "Paul was good to us. He packed you in ice, he helped us find the car."

"He had a candle lit before anyone else when the lights went out." Tad countered.

"And he left the silver candlestick holder in the garage."

"I forgot about that."

"It was valuable. Paul was in a hurry to get away with us, but he stopped to remove the candle, and leave the holder. Why would a thief do that?"

"I don't know," Tad admitted. "Hmm, He defended you against Lady Garmon's accusation. After he advised us both to keep quiet."

"There, you see?"

Tad shook his head. "Still, we can't rule him out, just because he's an underdog, and the most obvious. Just because we both hope he didn't do it. Linda, sometimes the obvious is just that. Once a thief—"

"Always a thief," she finished. "And the only good Indian is a dead Indian." She folded her arms.

Tad sat higher. They were beyond this, weren't they? "Quit that, Ahyoka."

Tears sprang into her eyes. "I am sorry!"

He breathed deeply, taking her hand in his. "We're both tired, I think. We had a rough night."

"I slept better with you beside me," she whispered.

"Maggie, too?"

"Sure. Maggie, too."

There, she smiled. But her voice still sounded sad to him. "People are not always as they seem, are they, Taddeusz?" she asked.

He felt his heart clench. "Not always."

"Paul Ferris is a caterer who is also Paul Ferradeau, a thief. Professor Adair is a wonderful teacher who is writing her doctoral thesis and is also an Irish nationalist, who wants that beloved island to become one country again. Dr. Milton is an environmentalist who is also..." Her voice faltered and Tad covered her hand with his. He wanted to make the last twenty-four hours disappear. She took a deep breath. "Even the Connor Emerald is transformed from sacred stone to centerpiece in a gaudy necklace."

"History," Tad said as he realized the link.

"History?"

"That's where the veils lift, Linda, when we dig into their past, their history. The emerald's history, too. It was part of Irish heritage first, until it got into English hands. We didn't know about the Connor Emerald's history until that run-in between the Garmons and Professor Adair. Maybe the stone itself is telling us to start with that."

"Start what?"

"Our way out of this mess. Come on, partner, what have we got?"

Linda smiled. "A patient with three taped up ribs who won't stay down. His inept keeper. Their guardian angel who would rather be trout fishing."

"I mean suspects!"

"Oh. Well, we have Professor Adair's list, with the names of everyone who attended the banquet."

"Right."

"Over two hundred names, addresses, phone numbers."

"Well, that narrows it down from everybody on the planet."

"I did not consider that."

"See? I'm good for something."

She rolled her eyes before opening her backpack and pulling out the computer sheets that Mary Adair had given them. Another compartment yielded a pencil.

"Let's zero in," Tad suggested, "on people we remember from last night."

She consulted the sheets. As her beautiful hair sifted, Tad caught a whiff of roses. "Besides Paul, Professor Adair and Dr. Milton, there were three members of the Garmon family."

"Lord Garmon. He seemed pretty decent to me," Tad offered.

"Except for the 'Red Indian' remark."

"Yeah, ignorant there, for all his refinement and manners. He seemed affectionate towards his wife."

"Was that real?"

"I know what you mean. What was real about last night? But he gave Lady Garmon the necklace. And he comforted her when it went missing. That was more than the son did. The son. What was his name?"

"Neil."

"Yeah. He was the one who gave me the feeling that the Garmons are not a happy family."

Linda sat up higher. "Tad. Neil was taken off the board of Garmon Chemicals last month."

"Was he?"

"I remember Dr. Milton talking about it. Some of the people at Walk With Wildlife were worried, because he was the board member most involved in the habitat project. He spoke up for our efforts, and had a lot of influence with his father. But that had been dwindling since his father married Lady Alice, they said.

"When they were at the habitat, there would be arguments, sometimes loud ones," Linda continued. And Neil almost disappeared since he was removed from the board of directors. We were worried. It was good to learn he had been invited to the banquet. We thought maybe they were patching things up."

"I wonder if Neil was in charge of the flowers."

"Why?"

"He taunted his stepmother with the admission that he took one for his lapel, didn't he? And the table was piled high with them. Who else got them? Were their cards unsigned too, like yours? I think we need to pay a visit to Nicos."

"Where?"

"Nico's of Buckhead. The florist."

"How did you remember that?"

"It was written on the box."

"And you have a photographic memory to compliment my phonograph one. What a team we are."

"Let's go."

"You still have thirty minutes resting time on the clock."

"Okay, coach," he said, defeated, as his hand found the stopwatch hanging from his neck. "Hey, guess what? I'm the coach."

"What are you saying?"

"I was offered a job." He pulled it out of his shirt for her to see. "Coach Nelson wants me to help train the volleyball team, when I'm feeling better."

"What an honor!" She narrowed her eyes. "But your position is not starting today."

"No, but I'm your coach."

"You make no sense, *unega,*" she insisted, giving him the Cherokee name for white man.

"Sure I do. The name of the thief is on that list, right?"

"Unless someone else sneaked in."

"Possible. But the security was pretty tight. And the police got there faster than we could get out."

"Tad. There is another way out. The Chatahoochee."

"Hey, that's right. And Dr. Milton is very familiar with that part of the river."

A mist seemed to descend on her. "Dr. Milton may be dead."

Tad took her arms in a gentle hold. "I'm not going to believe that until they find his body, Linda. This guy wasn't what he seemed. He liked to give expensive parties Mrs. Shaeffer said, remember? Maybe he had other expensive tastes. So, where did the money come from?"

"Theft? But there was not enough time, was there?"

"To grab the necklace, fake his own death, and get himself out, by way of the Chattahoochee? There's one way to find out. This stopwatch. Time it all out. Not just for Dr. Milton. For anyone with a reason to take that necklace."

"They will never let us back in. We are suspects ourselves."

"We can figure everything from right here. That's how I'm your coach, ready to run you through your paces. First, we figure out how long we were all in the dark before Lady Garmon knew her necklace was stolen."

"The call to the police came very fast— between the time we met Paul in the wine cellar and the police met us at the entrance."

"Yeah," Tad agreed. "Not much time for a thief to get to the riverbank. Ummm..."

"I know that thinking sound. 'Ummm ' what?"

"If that's where the thief went. Maybe he hid in the woods. Maybe he even stashed the necklace, or buried it."

"Oh, the poor animals and plants if people search for it. The habitat is over five hundred acres, Tad. Imagine the destruction. We must find that necklace!"

"Easy, love. Only Richard Wunder is unaccounted for, and we saw him escorted out before the theft."

"But he might have had a partner?"

"Sure. In fact, let's assume a partner, for all of them. Waiting by the river. How many steps to ground level from Lady Garmon in the big room?"

"One and a half stories."

Tad glanced around, saw the wide steps that led down to one of the park's playground areas. He nodded in their direction. "I can time you taking those seven steps, three times. That's a start."

"Yes. If it will keep you here, obeying your doctor." She pulled out a notebook and pencil from her backpack, and gave them to him. "You will need to figure out what shape each suspect is in for how fast the travel time. And footwear. And clothing."

"Me?"

"You are the numbers guy. I am your runner."

Tad enjoyed Linda's repeated runs so much he thought maybe it would not be so bad to help Coach Nelson out at volleyball practice. And maybe it would help him get along better with his teammates. Be more diplomatic, like Linda.

They tried to estimate the running times given extra weight, age, constrictive dress. Soon his mother's sweatsuit was shaping itself around Linda's curves. Tad watched as she splashed her face at the water fountain before her last run— playing Paul Ferris, who seemed in good shape and was close enough to their age that she could run as herself.

Afterward, she collapsed by his side. "What have you got?"

Tad looked at his stopwatch. "I forgot to press it down the second time," he admitted.

"Tad!"

"I was distracted."

"Distracted?"

"Well, you don't look anything like Paul Ferris."

"Men!"

Tad looked down at his figures. "I'll estimate."

Linda took a long drink from the Coke bottle she'd refilled with water. He calculated.

The results were disappointing. "All of them stay in the suspect category. Even Mary Adair in her long dress and high heels."

"Well, we learned things of value. A possible escape route. And that we might be looking for someone who hid the necklace. Or had an accomplice who escaped down the river. And, yes," she glanced at her watch and smiled. "You have fulfilled your doctor's orders."

Chapter 15

Linda put the car keys into her pocket and stood quietly at Tad's side in front of Nico's Florist, both armed with clipboards from the office supply store. They didn't make her feel confident. She associated flower sellers with bringing the joy in both distressed and happy times. Not deception.

They walked through the beveled glass doorway. Nico's was draped in sparkling gauze. Behind it, an army of silk and white dyed leather swans flew. More swans decorated the flower arrangements on display.

Linda and Tad had worked though their cover story until it was as close to the truth as possible. Now, would it succeed?

She introduced them both to the woman in the crisp white linen suit. "I work with the Walk With Wildlife project at Garmon Chemicals headquarters. I believe there were several orders—"

"What a tragedy! The Connor Emerald, lost! What will this do to Atlanta's reputation as an international trading center? The police must find the thieves soon. And isn't there someone missing? Or drowned?"

Linda looked away. Tad took over. "Yes, Ma'am. We're all very upset. But we're here about the roses. The order placed for honored guests?"

"Was there a problem with the roses?"

"Oh, no. They were perfect. What we need is a list of the persons they were sent to."

The woman's lips pursed. "Why?"

"The lottery," Linda offered.

"Lottery?"

"Oh, we were not supposed to call it that. What was the term, Tad?"

"Charity drawing donation," Tad said.

"Drawing, that's right. A drawing for," her eyes scanned the room, "lovely baby swans."

"They are cygnets."

"Of course. To represent the eggs hatching at the zoo in spring, you see. We would name one new cygnet for the recipient of each of the dozen roses. Once hatched, they are to be brought to the habitat and protected."

"What a very fine idea!" the woman gushed now, her suspicion evaporated.

Linda could no longer meet the florist's eyes.

Tad took up her story again. "Linda's too shy to tell you that she was one of those to be honored last night. But with Walk With Wildlife and Garmon Chemicals all caught up in the investigation, we volunteered to find the names of the other honorees. We don't want those eggs hatching without the sponsors knowing about it. If we show you this list of guests, could you possibly check your records for who were sent the roses?"

The woman took the clipboard from Tad's hands. "Of course."

Minutes later she returned with four purple stars now marking names on their list. "There you are. I will feel wonderful all day, knowing I helped four lovely swans find a home. But why didn't you ask the one who placed the order with us? The young man in the catering truck, with eyes to die for and lovely French manners."

"Paul Ferris," they both realized.

Tad's smile went crooked. "Paul was detained this morning. Well, Linda we've got to get these names to the zoo. Thank you, ma'am."

"Was I terribly obvious?" Linda asked.

"You were great. Besides, that lady had all her suspicions planted on me and my weather vane of a face. The swan lottery. Linda, that was perfect."

It is still hard to believe that Paul is involved in this."

"Maybe someone told him to place the order, that's all."

"I did not think of that."

"I didn't either, soon enough. If I had, I would have tried to get a look at who was billed for those flowers. I blew it."

"We both did. But we have the names."

"Thanks to your quick thinking about your save-the-swans cause."

"Oh, Tad, I feel awful."

"Why?"

"Because it was a lie, of course! And it came so easily."

He laughed.

"Stop that! When this is all over, can we adopt four cygnets at the zoo, to make that part true at least?"

"Sure."

Tad turned to her as they reached the car. "Does Paul Ferris really have eyes to die for?"

Linda felt a merry bubble forming inside her. It erupted in a flurry of giggles. She was beginning to wonder if she could make that sound again. Or feel the way she was feeling even toward this boy who walked in her soul. "Tad Gist," she summoned him. "I only have eyes for you."

"Yeah?"

No one was walking the elegant street, lined with trident maple trees. Linda felt Tad's hands circle her waist. Their first kiss was gentle and healing. The second went deeper and touched a place that sparked a flame and left them both without breath. Linda felt herself smiling as his warm lips descended a third time. Tad was a tall boy, and he must not strain his middle, she remembered, so she rose to her toes to share their third and best kiss.

A group of people turned the corner. Tad growled softly at their intrusion, but when they parted, he wore no traces of anger, only that sweet, dazed look she loved. He cupped the side of her face in his big gentle hand and kissed her forehead before he walked her to the driver's side of the car and opened the door for her.

Inside, they scanned Professor Adair's list in Linda's lap.

"Let's see who else our rose-giver marked with scent."

"Do you think that is why I received them, Tad? To be planted with suspicion?"

He shrugged. Linda caught his wince. He was hurting. And there was still an hour to go before he could swallow one of his pain relievers. She touched the place where his bandage was.

"I'm all right."

"No, you are not."

"I'm well enough, then. Let's find those names."

They searched for purple stars.

"Look. Maille Adair."

"So maybe she was supposed to smell like roses, too."

Tad frowned. "But she was not an original invited guest. Didn't she tell us that she got Dr. Milton to put her on the list?"

Linda nodded. "And she was not happy to be in his company, so I do not think they were from him. It was the Connor Emerald she wanted to see. Like Paul Ferris did. Only their reasons were different. She believes the stone belongs to Ireland."

"You're talking motive."

"True. Who else is on the list?"

"Richard Wunder."

"Richard Wunder? Why would roses be sent to a man who heads Wildlife First, an organization that wants to battle big business, not co-operate with them to benefit wildlife? I don't understand how he was even invited."

"And who invited him." Linda decided to voice her suspicion out loud. "A recently kicked-off-the-board son of a principle share holder?"

"Neil Garmon."

"He was the Garmon most involved in the sanctuary, Tad."

"And Wildlife First took responsibility for throwing paint on that opera diva's fur coat last year, remember? And for stealing a painting from the High Museum to draw attention to dolphin research. They break the law, Linda."

"Not a favorite party guest, then?" She flipped through the pages again. "No more purple stars."

"There's you."

"Okay. What is my motive?"

"To get those riverfront acres, by any means necessary. You've already gone through a lot of trouble for the environment. Your efforts got a dam stopped, remember? Troublemaker. I'm surprised they let you anywhere near Garmon's corporate headquarters."

"Tad Gist. You were involved in that dam prevention, as I recall."

"And whoever sent you the flowers might have known he was getting two suspects for the price of one."

"We are a bargain."

"Let's give Paul Ferris an honorary purple star."

"Why?"

"Part of his job was taking the flowers from the guests."

"Yes," Linda agreed. "He would end up scented."

"So, we've got the roses pointing at five of us: you and me, Maille Adair, Richard Wunder, and Paul Ferris."

"Because we're innocent, maybe they are too?"

"Not if one of them is the sender. I sure wish I'd looked at that bill at the—"he stopped himself suddenly, "Linda, start the car."

He covered his face with the side of his hand,

"Tad?"

"Please. Get us out of here."

Chapter 16

Tad rose slowly from his crouched position. He peered into the rearview window, hoping he could tell Linda some good news.

He could not. "Evasive maneuvers," he urged quietly.

"They are following us?"

"Yes."

"That is bad." She shifted her gaze to the car behind them. "And worse."

"Worse?"

"Diplomatic license plates. Immunity."

"From bad driving? Or causing fractured ribs?"

"Tad, do you think one of the men behind us hurt you?"

"Yes. Can you lose them?"

Tad saw her knuckles tighten as she gripped the steering wheel tighter. "Our best chance is on campus grounds, I think," she said, going over the speed limit to catch a yellow light, "I know those roads best."

Amid angry honking, the grey car behind them ran the red light.

They both approached the university entrance.

"No veering off onto bicycle paths," Tad warned.

"Hey. Who is driving?"

As Tad sighed, his taped up side felt sore, but not as bad as it had that morning. Was it getting better, or responding to his pain meds, or was adrenaline kicking into his system again? He was very thirsty. It must be the adrenaline.

Linda pulled onto the campus grounds. The grey car did not enter after them. She looped back around the main entrance's circle. Sure enough, the car was parked, outside.

"Maybe they think we're in another country," Tad suggested.

"One that would be harder on them than the Atlanta police? The FBI? The CIA?"

"Campus Security," Tad intoned gravely, "takes no prisoners."

Linda laughed. "I doubt they have that impression, but maybe they think this is also the only way out of the university grounds."

"It isn't?"

"No," she said as they pulled up to a parking space near her dormitory. "Okay. I think we are in a safe haven."

"Our own immune space?"

"Yes. Put your seat back and wait for me. You do not look well."

"I'm tired of hearing that."

"Shhh, pest," she said, kissing his cheek. "I am going to get things I need for tonight, and some water, for you. Then I am slipping us out and getting you home in one piece."

"You're a tough doctor."

"Not yet. But I may be, one day."

"I thought you were going into the foreign service? Or archeology?"

"Pre-med's starting to look easy. I will be right back."

Tad took two more of the coach's pain relievers with the thermos of water Linda brought out for him. Was she really thinking about pre-med courses? Was this experience enough to drive her out of international relations? Why couldn't he keep his eyes open?

He remembered leaving the Morris campus by a truck delivery entrance behind the Fine Arts building. He remembered thinking of Linda on the bicycle her family had provided, her strong legs pumping. She must have explored a lot of places he didn't even know about. He heard snatches of one of her Cherokee songs.

"Quit that," he murmured.

"You do not enjoy my singing?"

"Too soothing. It's putting me to sleep."

"That's the purpose of a lullaby, silly. No one is following us now. Go to sleep."

"But what if—"

"Rest your 'what ifs. 'Sleep."

Yeah, they must have lost those guys if Linda was singing, her knuckles relaxed. He could rest. Just for a minute.

Tad opened his eyes. He saw the leaves of a dogwood, then his sister Maggie waving a breeze from one of her dragon-painted fans in his face.

"Hey," he whispered hoarsely toward the Mercedes 'open sun roof, "get off my car."

"I won't dent it. I'm only forty-four pounds!" she said indignantly as she dangled down until their noses were almost touching.

"Cheeky possum."

"Sleepyhead," she retorted.

"I was just resting my eyes."

"Well, we're waiting supper."

"Supper?" He sat up slowly. "It's supper time? Where's Linda?"

"Coming, see?"

He turned to see Linda walking toward them. She had changed from his mother's sweat suit into a pretty earth-toned dress. Its knee length hemline caught a breeze as she walked.

"You look better," she said.

"You look beautiful."

"Why thank you, Tad."

Maggie rolled her eyes. Tad ran his hand through his hair. "Is it really suppertime?"

"Yes. Spinach lasagna."

"Wow. My mother only makes spinach lasagna on birthdays."

"Really? And your father is constructing the most interesting salad."

"Pineapple," Maggie informed him. "Daddy's putting pineapple in the salad."

"I must be an honored guest to merit birthday food and pineapples," Linda told them.

Tad waited until Maggie was busy gathering her drawings from under the dogwood tree before he lowered his voice. "Any signs of unwanted guests?"

"None."

Linda slipped her arm gently around his waist as they walked toward the house.

"Tell me why you suspect those men of the assault on your ribs."

He leaned his arm on the open porch's railing as they watched Maggie collect her art supplies. "It was the sound," he said.

"Sound?"

"Yes. Maybe I'm learning your phonograph memory. I've been trying too hard to remember what I saw that night before the lights went out. I didn't concentrate on what I'd heard. Coming up behind me. A halting kind of sound, with one foot coming down heavier than the other. I didn't remember it until I heard those people approaching us from behind at the florist. There were many footsteps, but that one was the loudest, the closest. Just like last night. Only now it was setting off a million alarm bells in my head."

"No wonder. But why do you think that man hit you, Tad?"

"Because they were part of the Liberian general's entourage."

"Bodyguards?"

"Judging from their size. When I was trying to get out to you, they blocked my path, because it would have crossed where the general was talking with Lady Garmon. They didn't understand much English.

137

That's why I jumped over the table. Maybe they still don't understand that I didn't mean anyone harm, I was just trying to reach you."

"But why would the heavy-footed man try to hit you afterward, when the lights went out? And why would he be following us now?"

"Hey, look Tad!" Maggie called out. "Where did you get these neat dolls?"

"Dolls?"

"Yeah...here in the trunk."

"She held up two carved figures pierced with feathers. One was shedding a yellow dust.

"Maggie!" Tad called out. "Put those down!"

Chapter 17

Linda caught up to Tad once his hurting side hobbled his stride. She'd never seen his face so full of fear. Not for himself. For Maggie. Linda reached into the car's trunk and pulled out a blanket. She looked up and saw Tad's love force back the fear.

"Put them here, Maggie," she instructed his sister gently.

The little girl, wide-eyed with surprise, did so. Linda placed the blanket holding the objects onto the grass.

"Her hands," Tad said between hard-won breaths. "Something's on her hands."

Linda stooped. Yellow dust clung to the little girl's palms.

"What's that?" Tad whispered.

"I think...yes, it is gold."

"Gold? Are you sure?"

"Tad. I come from the place where "there's gold in them there hills" originated, remember? I know what gold dust looks like."

"Wow. That's what's in your doll's hair, Tad," Maggie said.

"My doll?"

"Sure. This one is you, the other one is Linda," his sister explained patiently. "Who made them for you?"

Linda smiled. "That's what we would like to know."

"And why," Tad finished. He frowned at the carved dolls that were indeed their likenesses, down to tiny quill and bead earrings peeking out of Linda's black hair and his own slightly confused expression. The white and tiger-striped feathers sprouted from their shoulders like wings.

Maggie laughed. "They're presents. From someone who's sorry you got hurt, silly!"

"Tad!" his mother called from the porch doorway. "What's going on? Are you all right?"

Maggie winced. "I didn't mean to make you run and hurt yourself more."

"You didn't," he promised, ruffling her curls with the hand that wasn't holding his side. "Let's go inside and get you washed up."

"But I like them golden!"

"You can wash in a basin, and we'll save the gold," Linda assured her.

Linda felt the love of Tad's family encircle her as his mother and Dr. Gist sat with them on the floor of the house's screened in porch. Beyond them, in the back yard, Maggie swung from the branch of an old oak. Tad's attention kept wandering to her movements.

"She's all right, Tad," his mother assured him. "Let's brainstorm." She

140

centered all their attention back on the objects, now set out on a wicker picnic tabletop.

"Okay," Dr. Gist opened the discussion. "What are they?"

"Maggie says they're dolls. Of Linda and me. Do you think so?"

"Abstract, but possible," Kelsey Doyle speculated. "Made from mahogany, I'd say, right Stan?"

Her husband nodded his agreement.

"The clothing feels like cotton."

"The 'Linda 'is wearing red, as she was last night," Dr. Gist observed.

Kelsey leaned over for a closer look. "And you're painted in penguin black and white, like your tux. I understand Linda's tiny earrings, and Tad's hapless eyebrows, but why all the feathers?"

"Feathers are important to the Cherokee," Linda offered. They are links to the birds, which are messengers from Skyland."

"I wonder if the people from western Africa feel a similar link," Dr. Gist said. "If the men you had a run in with last night were from Liberia, and they put the dolls in your trunk, perhaps it was a way of—"

"Laying a curse on us? Voodoo or something?" Tad asked.

"Or apologizing," Linda countered his fear.

They all turned to her.

"Apologizing?"

"Yes," she said calmly. "For hurting you. Perhaps it was a misunderstanding."

"Linda, they followed us all over town, remember? They ran a red light to keep up."

"And we did not stop, turn around to ask them why. They are guests in our country. Chief Hawes said they needed two translators to make themselves understood, and to understand. They are more afraid of us than we are of them, maybe."

Linda watched Tad's hand move to protect his side. Was she causing this boy she loved more pain?

His mother shook her head as if Linda had voiced her thought out loud. "He gets surly when he's hungry. Punch up Liberia on our "Countries of the World" disk, Stan, while Linda and I make a salad and put out the lasagna. Linda's right. The least we can do is get a better idea of the people with whom we might be dealing. We'll discuss your findings over dinner."

Dr. Gist grinned. "Are we slipping into traditional gender roles?"

His wife frowned. "Just slipping into the kitchen—still a sacred place for girl talk. If you two want to eat, you'd better be ready with a full report."

Linda followed Tad's mother. She liked how Kelsey Doyle accepted her help and the quiet hum of the cheerful kitchen.

"I'm glad this is my day off at the network, Linda. Calling in favors has kept me almost as busy."

"Favors?"

"From fellow reporters who have been working on the Connor Emerald story. And a few sources at the police department. I'm glad you met with Chief Hawes."

"Detective."

"Oh, of course, detective, here in Atlanta. He was a real advocate for you and Tad last night. I'd put my hand in the fire for that man."

Linda nodded. "I would too."

"I talked with Grace Monahan too. The policewoman?"

Linda stared down at the knife she was using to chop carrots for the family's salad. "Deputy Monahan was very kind," she whispered.

"Linda, I asked her if she knew why you might be having nightmares."

Linda put down the knife.

"I heard you screaming last night. When I came to check on you, Tad was already there. In your bed, in fact."

Linda felt her face heat with embarrassment. "Tad and I, we did not—I mean, we were not—"

"Oh, I know that, sweetie. Tad was settling you so nicely. And you trusted in his comfort, I could see that. I was proud of my son."

"Good." Linda nodded, relieved. "That's good."

She placed the carrots into the salad bowl, already filled with romaine lettuce, green onions, and chopped tomatoes. She caught the scent of Kelsey Doyle's honeysuckle cologne.

"Are you feeling better today?" she asked quietly.

Linda nodded and felt a carefully manicured finger sift back a strand of her hair over her shoulder. "You were very brave to have made a statement about Dr. Milton."

Linda nodded. The salad was done. Set the table. Utensils. Five forks. Keep moving she told her freezing brain. Kelsey brought out the trivets for the lasagna and the hot garlic bread.

"Linda, Deputy Monahan believes you. We all believe you."

Linda raised her eyes to the woman with kind eyes standing across the dining room table. "You do?"

"Of course."

"Why do I not remember it better, Ms. Doyle?"

"Perhaps you had to shut down a little. To recover. Others have stepped forward to back up your claims about the man."

"What do you mean?"

"Our education reporter, he and I have been in touch. He's been on the Morris campus all day. Complaints against Dr. Milton's behavior toward female students are being unearthed. Six women, four former undergraduates and two graduate students have lodged new accusations of sexual harassment."

"They have? Six?"

"So far. Your bravery is contagious, it seems. If he shows up, I think Dr. Milton will find himself fired, tenured or not."

"If he shows up. If he is alive."

"True. The Chattahoochee has a tendency of keeping secrets for a while." An impish look suddenly transformed Tad's mother's face. "But they say only the good die young, don't they?" she confided with a smile that quirked one side of her mouth up. "This has not been a great introduction of college life for you, Linda. Or to Atlanta's thriving corporate or international relations life."

"You have heard from your sources about that?"

"Yes. Our business reporter had a stack of paperwork on the Garmons. Much of it is the corporate stereotype on both sides of the Atlantic— Neil Garmon, furious when Father abandons Mother for a trophy wife."

"Trophy?" Linda asked, confused.

"Younger, glamorous, an arm piece to show off. The new Lady Garmon's beat used to be California. Her first husband was a movie actor, the second, a director. Maybe Lord Garmon was her bid for lasting security. Married only eighteen months, but long enough to get into three public rows with her stepson. Two in Britain, one here in Atlanta, after which he was thrown off Garmon's board of directors and, rumor has it, disinherited."

"What a family out of balance," Linda said sadly.

"Yes. And the marriage might be cracking, my sources say. Alice Garmon's cultivated accent is a sham. She isn't a member of the upper classes that she pretends to be. The necklace became a joke in the British tabloids—the famed Connor Emerald being reset by a lower-class playgirl. Lord Garmon hoped it would make her more acceptable, and keep the peace between them."

"But the stone has had nothing but strife connected to it for generations! Why would Lord Garmon choose the Connor Emerald to make peace?"

"Oh, Linda. Most people don't see the deeper layers of history the way you do. They're caught in the surface sparkle."

"Is that why it is so hard for me to understand these things?"

"You're not the only one. Our business reporter complains about how his job did not used to include knowing where 'the Donald ' and Rupert Murdoch and the Garmons dined, fought and skied. He still isn't used to covering business summits in the company of reporters from entertainment TV shows."

As Kelsey Doyle spoke, Linda felt trapped in a prism of light and color that was the Connor Emerald.

Chapter 18

Tad looked across the dining room table at Linda, happy to see her enjoying his mom's lasagna.

"It looks like we've discovered our gift givers," his father announced.

"What did you find, Stan?" his mom asked.

"All the components of the figures: iron, mahogany and gold, are products of Liberia."

"What about local customs, Dr. Gist?" Linda asked. "They may help to tell us if we are under a blessing or a curse."

"Not much explained in that area, I'm afraid. Liberia's government was dominated by descendants of enslaved Americans that had acquired their freedom. That is, until the military took over in 1980. Africans without American-born family lines make up ninety per cent of the population. They speak many different languages. It's no wonder the police are having a hard time with their interviews, just with the general and his bodyguards alone! The population includes Christians, Muslims, and many who practice the local nature-based religions that honor ancestors and the spirits in animals, trees, rocks. That last might be the traditions of our

147

gift-givers, I'd say. We didn't find anything more specific."

Tad's mother broke a crusty piece of garlic bread. "I think you'd better show your gifts to Detective Hawes."

"Sure, Mom. We have a meeting with him tonight at Mitchell's."

Linda raised her brows slightly, but gave no other indication that this was the first time she was hearing about this appointment. Tad was counting on that.

"Mitchell's? Not too late tonight, I hope," Kelsey said.

"Bring me home a treat, Tad?" Maggie asked.

"It may be too late to catch you before bedtime, Sprite. But we'll bring home something you can have tomorrow, how's that?"

"And the story of your dolls too?"

Linda smiled. "If we know it, we will tell it," she promised.

Linda waited to question Tad until they had said goodbye to his family and were in the car.

"I did not know you scheduled a meeting with Detective Hawes."

"I didn't."

But Tad, you told your parents—"

"I said we'd meet him there."

"And will we?"

"Sure. I'll phone him. After we've looked around and asked a few of our own questions. Linda, what if Detective Hawes jumps to the same conclusions that I did about the dolls? That they're some kind of revenge, or a curse?"

"You do not think that now?"

"Let's say I'm open to other possibilities."

"Ones that do not include a Liberian general and his bodyguards as enemies?"

"We sure don't need to add to our combustibles of family squabbles, animal rights activists, and Irish politics."

"Hmmm. Maybe it is related. Maybe the Liberian general is Black Irish," Linda said, eyes on the road, face forward. Tad looked more closely to catch the slight quirk around her mouth. Her relatives at the Snowbird reservation expressed humor in the same dry manner.

Tad groaned. "Hey. Don't make the patient laugh. It hurts when he laughs."

Linda's brows slanted with her concern.

"Now I'm joking Ahyoka, don't worry."

Linda didn't laugh. She looked at her watch.

"I took my medicine with dinner, remember? Don't get over protective now...I'll need you on my side when W.C. Hawes finds out about our left-in-the-trunk gifts."

"He is our friend, Tad. And we cannot tell him about our gifts without telling him about the men who followed us."

"How about...only if he asks?"

"We must tell him everything."

"Even if it cramps our own efforts?"

"Yes."

"A compromise. We call him after we do two things: meet with Professor Adair, and check if our stopwatch timing confirms our estimates at Garmon Headquarters?"

"After Professor Adair only. It is getting dark." Her eyes scanned the rearview mirror.

"See anyone?"

"No. Just a feeling. Foolish."

"There's nothing foolish about you, Linda."

Professor Adair's apartment was in an early twentieth century structure holding out against a more expensive, modern apartment buildings and office complexes. The neighborhood's mix of Korean and Middle Eastern eateries and Irish pubs reminded Tad that Atlanta was not a typical Southern city.

They knew something was wrong as soon as the elevator doors opened on their teacher's floor. Her apartment door was slightly ajar. Tad nudged the door open further with his foot.

"Professor Adair?" Linda called softly inside as they entered.

The living room was in shambles—books pulled off their shelves, pillows and seat cushions yanked from furniture. A large painting of a pastoral countryside was on the floor with a message spray painted green where it had been on the wall: *Beidh ar LaLin.* In English, below it, in black: We will have our day.

Linda grabbed Tad's hand. "I smell smoke," she said.

Chapter 19

They backed out of the apartment and closed the door. "I saw a fire extinguisher by the elevator," Linda said. "I will get it."

"Okay. I'll look for a fire alarm."

"Good. Pull it and wait for me. Do not go back into that apartment alone, Tad, promise me."

"Promise."

It took three tries to get the extinguisher from the wall. Linda read the label. It was a multipurpose dry chemical type. Good, she thought, remembering from her emergency assistance training. This kind could be used to put out combustible materials, gasses, liquids, or electrical equipment.

The building's fire alarm sounded. Tad had found it. She raced back towards Professor Adair's apartment, hoping nothing had tempted him to go inside.

He was waiting, his arms tense, his fingers twitching. "Smoke's worse," he said.

She pulled the lapels of his denim jacket up over this throat and nose. Then she pulled her own sweater collar higher. Tad took her hand before they made their way over the room's broken furniture and toward a hallway. The smoke was coming from under the second door.

Tad touched it. "Hot."

Linda swept the light curls off his sweat-lined brow.

"Ready?" he asked her.

"Yes."

She opened the door slowly. Orange flames danced up from a bed. The fire had spread to the curtains at a double window, one wall, and was eating up papers and the top of a desk nearby. The plastic case of Professor Adair's Macintosh Classic II computer was melting, as was an electrical outlet.

Tad pulled the locking pin from the fire extinguisher as Linda released the hose and nozzle from their clasp. Tad pressed the handle. A stream of pressurized powder spewed in the direction of the bed, then the computer, where Linda thought the hottest part of the fire was. Smoke seared at her lungs through the scant protection of her raised collar.

She looked up. Tad's eyes were tearing. She reached over and released more powder along the wall and curtains.

The flames died down, then went out.

Linda took Tad's hand. "We need better air. We must get out."

They opened all doors of the hallway's three rooms—a bathroom and another bedroom and on their way out, looking and calling for their teacher. But there was no sign of Professor Adair.

When they reached the ransacked living room, a group of three, two men and a woman, appeared in the smoky mist.

A guy in a black T-shirt stepped forward. "Is it out?" he asked Tad.

"We think so. Tad surrendered the fire extinguisher to him. "Here. In case it flares up."

"Ta," the man said.

Linda heard the wail of an approaching fire engine.

"The tenants are all getting outside, the woman of the group informed them. "Anyone else here? The professor?"

"We didn't find her. We are her students. We had an appointment to meet with her and found...this."

The woman scanned the living room. "Aye. Looks like someone got here first."

"The IRA?" the t-shirted man asked her and their still silent companion.

"I'm thinking, no," the woman said. "Took time for a proper English translation. But *linn*'s got a double n, you see? Even the poorly schooled in Irish know that."

Linda thought of Professor Adair's words. Set up. Framed. Who was doing this? Why were she and Tad being pulled in? What else did Mary Adair know to make her so dangerous as to risk the lives of everyone in her apartment complex?

Tad glanced out the window at the flashing lights of the fire trucks. "We've got to go," he told the trio. "We'll tell the fireman the apartment number."

"Three-twenty-three, lad," the silent man finally spoke, taking the fire extinguisher under his arm.

"Yes, sir. And thanks for standing by." Tad took Linda's hand and headed for the stairs.

Soon they began mingling with the last of the exiting tenants. Tad passed the word of the fire's location among them before he and Linda slipped out a back door and away from the flashing vehicles.

Linda noticed a hitch in his stride. "Slow down!" she pleaded.

"We can't. Whoever's trying to frame Professor Adair, they've got her, or she's in hiding. Linda, they won't stop. And they may be after us, too."

"Who are they?"

"Irish nationalists?"

"But they can't spell!"

"The Liberians, then? Trying to look Irish?"

"If we explain to the police—"

"No, not the police. Just Chief Hawes, he'll understand."

Tad finally stopped so abruptly that Linda ran into his back. She steadied herself with a hold at his shoulder. He stood still, blocking her view of something. Then he turned. Slowly.

"Tad," Linda whispered. "Let me see."

He stood aside. Tad's car was spray-painted with the same green and black as Professor Adair's living room. Shards of window glass lay scattered on the street. The trunk of the Mercedes was open, and their feathered likeness dolls were on the ground, burning like small torches. A crowd was gathering around, murmuring. A few shook their heads. A few more were signaling to an approaching police officer.

Linda grasped Tad's hand. "There's a transit station close."

They backed up, turned, linked arms, and walked quickly toward the lighted MARTA sign and stairs.

The downtown Atlanta rush hour was over, but the trains were still arriving frequently. In the reflection of a platform's advertisement featuring Alex Trebek asking 'got milk?' with his whitened mustache, Linda noticed Tad's eyes darting in confusion. She nodded towards an incoming train. "This one will bring us to the Five Points Station, right across from the entrance to Underground Atlanta."

He smiled. "How'd you get to be such a city girl?"

"No car, remember?"

They got on the train. Linda realized the other passengers were staring at them. Linda took a good look at Tad in the harsh lighting of the train's interior. He was covered in a layer of black ash. From his wide-eyed stare, she realized that so was she. The fire had marked them.

"Do you have a handkerchief?"

He reached into his back pocket and handed her the neatly folded white square. "Don't spit on it," he warned.

She laughed. "It's loose soot mostly. I think we can dust it off.

He cleaned her face as gently as she cleaned his. "Hmm," she judged as he worked, "I can tell I am not your first sullied date."

"Well, Maggie likes chocolate. Sometimes we have to hide the evidence from Mom."

"I am sorry about your car, Tad."

He shrugged as he stuffed his handkerchief into his back pocket. He did both without wincing, even after their walk and stair journey. He was healing, despite the day they had had, Linda realized.

"Could have been worse," he reflected now. "They might have lit the car on fire, the way they did our figurines." He sighed. "Maggie liked those dolls."

Linda thought of the two artifacts burning in the street. He was right. Whoever had done that had the time to be even more destructive. Were the dolls burned to make them feel as she was feeling now: warned? Stay away. Stay out of this.

They must be getting closer to some answers.

When they emerged from the Five Points station, Linda realized that downtown looked very different after dark. The atmosphere was more festive, less businesslike. Couples—tourists, office workers, a few waiters and waitresses changing shifts, musicians with cased instruments under their arms—were all entering the network of streets known as Underground Atlanta.

Her people had history here. Lower Alabama Street was the original Underground location, existing since before the Civil War, when streets were built over railroad tracks that converged at the heart of the city. The Cherokee had a trading terminus here long before then. That history, told to her by her grandmother, was what first brought Linda to the carefully restored historic buildings below the streets of the twelve-acre urban space.

By night the district became an entertainment center. Tad and Linda walked past specialty shops, restaurants and nightclubs from which music from bluegrass to New Orleans inspired Dixieland to rock sang out the doors and into the street. Texas two- step clop competed with Beach Boys harmonies.

"Are we in a time warp?" Tad asked.

"Maybe we are on the holodeck of Captain Picard's ship."

Tad laughed and squeezed her hand. Since her dorm mates had introduced her to the episodes of The Next Generation, they were both fans of this newer version of the Star Trek series.

Still, Linda felt more at home in an archeological dig than this bustling version of a holodeck. Here times and cultures went by too fast, too out of balance. There were no children or families, and everyone seemed at least a decade older than they were. It was still early in the evening, but people around them were drinking too much alcohol already.

"We don't exactly fit in with this crowd," Tad observed.

Linda wound her arm around his waist. "And as W. C. Hawes might say, '"Why aren't you two at home writing a paper'?"

"Yeah, why aren't we?" Tad asked, sounding tired.

"Mitchell's is not far. We can call the chief from there, and wait for him."

"Right. Good plan."

As they passed one of Underground Atlanta's antique gas lamps, it flickered.

"Did you see that?" Tad asked.

"Ghosts?"

"Of whom?"

"Former caretakers of the Connor Emerald?"

"I hope they're with us tonight."

"They are with us, Tad." Saying it almost made Linda believe it. "We both have Irish relatives."

"Your dad's side, and my mom's," he remembered. "You're right."

Mitchell's was like a haven of simple dining amid the more sophisticated night life of Underground Atlanta. Linda looked past the booths done up in oilcloth to the bright red Coca-Cola vending machine and jewel-toned juke box. There—the old wooden phone booth in the back was what they needed now. She headed for it as Tad nodded toward Gus Mitchell. The handsome African American man with the grin showing off his gold tooth as he returned the greeting, although he was busy supervising a younger man as they put together a large take-out order.

Linda tried to enjoy the familiar warmth of the place, decorated in a decade that her own parents could barely remember—the 1950s. But now the times she'd been here with Dr. Milton and her fellow students took on a new, more sinister light. They found a booth and slid in. Concentrate on getting information about her teacher and the red-haired woman, Linda told herself. According to Chief Hawes, they came here late at night.

"Shall I make the call to the chief?" Tad asked.

"Would you mind? I want to look around, and talk with Mr. Mitchell."

"You're better at both." He flipped her a quarter. "Play 'Wake Up Little Susie 'for me?"

160

"Sure."

Linda smiled. The song was theirs now, ever since he had sung it to keep her awake during a middle-of-the-night drive.

As she turned to the juke box, Linda watched Tad open the door of the phone booth and slip inside. She enjoyed reading over the names of the old rock and roll songs. Yes, the selection included four Everly Brothers 'tunes, among them 'Wake Up Little Susie. 'She punched in the number of her selection.

As ragged a couple as they made after the fire sooted their hair, skin and clothing, Linda would not have chosen to be anywhere else or in anyone else's company. The 45 rpm record flipped onto the turntable and the song began. Tad turned toward the sound and placed his palm against the glass door. He smiled at her.

His smile made Linda feel like a pear ripening in the summer sun, proud and protected and very alive. She shook her head, chastising herself. Was being in this much trouble, even with this boy who makes her heart sing, her idea of a good time?

She approached the phone booth as Tad opened the accordion fold door.

"Get through?" she asked.

He groaned. "On hold."

He pulled her into the booth with him. Yes, Linda thought as he kissed her: a pear, ripening. How had this white boy learned such love medicine?

She heard a tinny voice from the now dangling phone receiver.

Tad recovered it. "Yes, Ma'am," he answered the voice. "I know he's retired from the force, but he's working on a special—listen, is Deputy Grace Monahan there? Sure, I'll wait."

He took the phone from his ear and kissed her nose. "Hey," he called softly. "We're steaming up the booth. Look, Gus is waving you over. Go, be your diplomatic self as you grill him."

As she approached, Linda knew introductions would not be necessary. "You came here over the summer with the wildlife group, didn't you?"

"Yes, sir. My name is Linda Tassel."

"Nice to know your name. You stepping out with our Tad now, Linda?"

"Stepping out?" She should know what that meant. She suddenly felt strange without Tad beside her. She looked to the phone booth. He was deep in conversation. Stepping out sounded like something good, so she said, "Yes."

"Well, that's fine! He's a good one. And you know Chief W. C. Hawes, he told me that when he picked up some ice cream and brought me in on your case. Good man, the chief, with smart kids—doctors and lawyers and such. It's all because of my ice cream, he tells me. So he had to get you and Tad off on your college days in the right way. How's progress? You have any questions for me?"

"Why, yes, sir."

"Well, you'll never guess who just left in a taxi."

"Dr. Milton?" Linda asked, hoping against hope that he was ready to be alive and end her nightmare."

"No. His redheaded lady friend."

"The one he brought here at night?"

"Exactly. W.C. told you about her?"

"Yes, sir."

"She must have had a few, she was weaving. Then, oh the scene! We just finished cleaning up from her before you came in."

"Please tell me about this, Mr. Mitchell."

"Well, she wore the same kind of flashy clothes from the times she came in with Dr. Milton. She sat in a booth for a while, just staring at the condiments. Then she went to the juke box, playing every Elvis song we've got. Then she went for our Coke machine."

"Went for?"

"Like it was her enemy! I thought she was trying to put money in it. I tried to explain to her that it was not a vending machine now—that we modified it to be a cooler. 'Well, where is the ice? 'she demanded. I lifted the top to show her. Well, she dug through it, screaming like the hounds of hell were after her."

"Screaming what, sir?"

"Let me think. She was hard to understand. Something about a plan ruined because he couldn't keep it in his pants.

'Nobody can keep ice in pants for long 'I tried to josh her out of it, you know? Well, it set her off again, laughing this time. Almost laughed that wig off her head."

"Her red hair was not real?"

"No. It fell away from the black band holding it on until she caught it, pushed it back, and dug through my ice supply some more. My, my, I thought she was going to fall in herself, before she sure enough found something."

"What?"

"Paper, with writing on it, in a plastic baggie, that leaked. I guess it was clear enough, though the paper was limp, because her lips moved as she read it. Well, that quieted her down. She asked Vince to call her a cab. Vince was happy to do it, because she'd sure cleared half our customers out."

"Where was she going?"

"Argued with the cab service, we all could hear that! Vince gave her the house phone. Hey Vince," Mr. Mitchell called over a young man who was returning from behind a curtain. "Did the lady say where she was heading?"

"Promised to cover his return to the city," Vince offered. "From that place you all worked at all summer—the wildlife place on the Chatahoochee."

Mr. Mitchell came closer. "You hungry, young one? Let me fix you up something, you look worn out. Tad's off the phone now. Look after your girl, son."

Tad's hand grabbed hers. "We have to go. Now."

Chapter 20

"Hey," Gus Mitchell called behind them, "Where are you off to?"

"Home," Tad said over his shoulder, "if my folks call, sir." Then whispered. "Eventually."

"You have turned red, weathervane," Linda said quietly as their footsteps sounded on the cobblestone street outside the ice cream parlor. "I do not think that was the whole truth."

Tad put his arm around her. "Linda. There are two guys under that lamppost. With familiar faces. And fists."

"General Tenatu's bodyguards?"

"And more at the exit doors."

"Not all of the exit doors."

"What do you mean?"

"Come. My friend Alison works in the food court. I know a service way out." She led him on a zig-zag route through where a crowd had gathered to watch a street performer and his magic act. Tad looked for General Tenatu's men. His side ached but soon they were in a corridor between a frozen yogurt shop and Just Fries. The smell made his stomach rumble.

Linda stopped. "Tad, we have to go through here."

He looked up at the sign on the door: Women.

"I can't! Maybe there's a way outside the men's room, too?"

"Maybe. But the men's room is on the other side of the food court. Please, Tad."

Linda's hand suddenly went to her throat. Tad turned. Four guys were coming down the corridor. In a hurry. He grabbed Linda and they barged in through the door together. The pink tiled blur went by so fast that Tad hardly registered a few girls changing into their fast-food employee uniforms. But real screeches of protest started once they were out the door and onto Alabama Street.

"The men. They are following us," Linda said.

As the mounting pain slowed his progress toward the MARTA station stairs, Tad thought about telling Linda to go on alone.

"We are doing fine," she insisted. She unzipped the side section of her backpack, slipped out two copper coins, then took a stronger hold on his arm. Tad felt himself collapsing. She would never be able to hold him. But she slipped the tokens in the turnstile, and yanked him through.

"Only the stairs are left," she told him.

The stairs. Of course. He could do stairs, where gravity was on his side. If those purple spots would just get out of the way. He stumbled on the last three, but she caught him. Then she flung them both through an open door of a waiting train car.

"You're stronger than you look," Tad gasped out as the doors closed.

"*Hi hwi lo hi*!" she commanded, nodding toward an empty seat.

He thought he recognized the command she used with her family's dog. "Hey, are you putting me in a corner?"

"Yes. Sit!"

He crashed into the seat with a disgruntled sigh, breathing heavily. Linda stood over him, keeping watch at the window. She didn't sit beside him until the train was on its way.

"They did not have travel tokens, I think," she said.

"Which you always carry?"

"Of course. I am a city person with—"

"No car. I've heard."

She put her hand against his sore ribs. Tad closed his eyes and leaned against the seat back in the empty train car. "So, city person, where are we headed?"

"The end of the line. But then we have another three miles to go. You cannot walk that far." She dug into her backpack and drew out her wallet. "I have seven dollars. How much do you have? How much do taxis cost?"

"Hold on. Where are we going?"

"To Garmon Headquarters."

The scene of the crimes. Tad winced.

"We have to, Tad. She is on her way there. "

"Linda. That might not be a good idea, I have to tell you about my phone call. What I learned back there at Mitchell's."

"All right. We will listen to each other, and then decide. Agreed?"

"Agreed."

"I talked to Deputy Monahan," Tad began.

"She is a good person. And courageous."

"Courageous, all right. To offer the advice she did when I was handing her over the police's prime suspect without even knowing it."

"You were?"

"They've got an arrest warrant. And an all-points bulletin out."

"On whom?"

"You."

"This is not a good time to joke, Tad."

"I know that, love."

"How did they decide this?"

"Direct testimony. From an eyewitness. Deputy Monahan explained that they finally cracked a language barrier between them and the witness. That's why Chief Hawes was not at the station when I called—he'd put himself in charge of apprehending you."

"Tad, what are we going to do?"

"Stay out of the way of that warrant. I think that's what Deputy Monahan was saying in her roundabout secret code way.

My parents knew we planned to meet W. C. at Mitchell's, remember? If he called my house to find our whereabouts, they'd send him right to you."

"If he wanted to catch me."

"You don't think he does?"

"No."

"Linda, the man's got a job to do."

"Which does not include hunting someone down who he knows did not take that necklace."

"Maybe you're right. But we can't hide forever. We've already got General Tenatu's bodyguards looking to settle some score we don't know anything about. Professor Adair makes an appointment with us then gets her apartment trashed and burned. We haven't been exactly invisible."

"The black band. Oh, Tad, could it be?"

"Wait. Could what be?"

"At the banquet, remember? Professor Adair wore a black band in the hair."

"Sure, why?"

"So did the red-haired woman."

"Professor Adair has dark hair."

"Which can be covered with a wig."

"Linda. We both know how good Professor Adair is with accents and voices from the wonderful way she taught our Celtic Studies class. Was she going with Dr. Milton again? In some sort of disguise?"

"She could shape shift into anyone. But, oh Tad, I like Professor Adair. Even thinking of her as a liar or a thief is hard for me."

He draped his arm across her shoulder. She snuggled into his good side, her cedar scent coming through. Was the scent part of her body chemistry? If he could just close his eyes for a minute... No, he mustn't sleep. Think.

"Lots of women wear those headbands. Come on, Linda, let's think. Other possibilities? Hey, did Gus or Vince say their madwoman had eyes to die for?"

"Tad, what are you saying?"

"Only that Paul Ferris has a slight build, is clean shaven, and might have been in disguise."

"But Paul's in jail."

"Not since the warrant for you was secured."

She sat up, frowning. "All right. Let's consider. Paul had opportunity."

"And motive. His family's line of work. Plenty of fencing of the necklace possibilities."

Linda's frown deepened. "What about the Garmons?"

"Unless you think Lord Garmon or his son would also look good in a dress, there's only one woman in that family, and she's the victim."

"Do you think it was Lady Garmon who named me as the thief, Tad?"

Tad thought back to his phone discussion. "I admit I didn't get a clear idea from the crazy roundabout talk I had with Deputy Monahan. Maybe we'd better not get too crazy about the identity of our lost-in-the nineteen-fifties woman and concentrate on her connections."

Linda lifted her head higher. "Lost in the fifties."

"Yeah, sitting in a booth out of Happy Days, playing old Elvis songs, you know?"

"Tad. It is what Mr. Mitchell said to Chief Hawes this afternoon. About Dr. Milton. That he was lost in the nineteen-fifties."

"Yeah. So?"

"I have never thought of Dr. Milton as connected with the necklace."

"But now this woman of his connects him."

"I was too respectful. Not wanting to slander the dead. Too respectful of him, again. Yes, this woman now connects him to the Connor Emerald. We must find her, Tad."

He sighed. "Well, Atlanta traffic being what it isn't, I'd say we might get to Garmon Headquarters ahead of her."

Linda gave him a small smile. Then she stared into her lap. As privileged as Tad felt to be granted this window into a vulnerable part of her, it made him angry to think of her in fear. They had to reach the wildlife habitat and make the woman tell them what was going on. And why Linda was getting the blame. This nightmare had to end, now. He pulled her close. A soft Cherokee lullaby began flowing through her.

"Stop," he demanded weakly, holding his head in his hands.

"Hush now," she whispered, before starting another verse.

Chapter 21

As the train glided on, Linda was grateful for the smooth ride that allowed Tad to sleep. She'd always brought her bike for the last of the way to the wildlife habitat, but had noticed taxicabs waiting at many different times at the MARTA stop. She needed one now because Tad should walk as little as possible

She could see Tad's reflection in the train window's glass. His unruly curls danced with the rocking. He was still sleeping, caught in the spell she'd made with her lullaby. Was there anything wrong with him beyond soreness and fatigue? She imagined his cracked ribs pulling apart, their edges sharp and deadly, ready to rupture his lung. Away! She commanded that vision, born of her fear. She replaced it with one of the bones knitting together, stronger than before. And the ugly purple bruising turned yellow, then blended in with his skin's tone.

"Last stop!" the train's conductor announced on the intercom.

Tad didn't move.

She touched his shoulder. "Wake up, Camellia Man."

His eyes, the color of mountain columbine, appeared startled. Then he looked out the window of the train's car. "You've got a pretty sorry guardian angel." He pulled his hand through his hair. "I hope I can do better by you this time," he said sadly.

"Oh, Taddeusz." She kissed his cheek. "What is better than perfect?"

Linda was glad there was a taxi waiting at the station. The day had taken its toll on both of them, but she was more concerned about Tad. When she learned that the ride was going to cost less than the money they'd pooled together, she ran to a vending machine and bought a can of Coca-cola ®.

He took it with a smile and pressed it against his side. "Ah."

Linda giggled. "When you have finished wearing it, drink up."

He made a disgusted face. "Didn't the machine have mineral water?"

"Mineral water does not contain caffeine."

"I had my nap. And I'm a night person, remember?"

"We'll share it," she compromised as she opened the cab door. "Get in."

The driver turned around after she told him their destination. "You kids sure you want to go to the Garmon Headquarters? They probably won't let you in."

"But we're with the wildlife habitat," Linda tried.

"And there's a meeting tonight," Tad finished, figuring there would be, once they caught up to the red-haired woman.

The driver, a broad-faced, mustached man in a tweed cap, stopped at a red light and again looked back over his shoulder. "You know about the big to-do, then? Lady Garmon having her necklace stolen during that big deal party?"

"Yes, we know about it," Tad offered.

"But maybe you don't know that it's you wildlife people that Garmon is keeping out now."

"What do you mean, sir?" Linda asked him.

"The investigation has really messed with the running of the place. You know—police all around, detectives going through files and records. Garmon's beefed up his own security, to keep out looky-loos and reporters. One of the guards told me there's strict instructions to keep the wildlife people out. Seems Garmon thinks they're behind his wife's losing that necklace and the guy drowning. Sounded nutty to me."

Linda gasped. "Drowning? Have they found Dr. Milton?"

"Not yet. But he's down there. This part of the Chattahoochee hides bodies for weeks, months. That drunk woman who missed a curve back in '88? A year to the day they found her in her little sports car, pretty as you please, still behind the steering wheel. Well, maybe not so pretty by then. That professor is down there all right, feeding the fish."

Linda shivered. Tad took her hand, squeezed. That was what she needed to be able to think again.

"Would you bring us to the park? The one that's north of Garmon Headquarters? Walk With Wildlife has an office there. It is a small cottage, near the playground."

"Oh, yeah, I know the place. You folks took my youngest's cub scout troop on a hike from there. Sure, I can drop you off."

"Thank you."

"You got a jacket in that pack? Supposed to go down in the forties tonight."

"We both do, thanks."

She was touched by the driver's concern, but it became a problem when they drove up to the small riverfront park.

"There are no lights on in the building," he observed. "You sure you're in the right place?"

Tad to the rescue. "Sure. We're just early for the meeting."

"Still, I hate to leave you here. In the dark."

"There's a pay phone, beside the cottage, see?"

The driver reached into his shirt pocket and pulled out a business card. "Well, all right, then."

Linda took it. "We'll call if we need a ride back to the station," she assured him.

"Put those jackets on, hear?"

177

"We will, sir," Tad said, placing his arm around Linda's shoulder as they watched the taxi driver head down the road.

"We must look pretty pitiful."

"I think it is more than that," Linda said quietly. "Our kind driver sensed something. You do too, Tad."

"What?"

"Something out of balance. Dangerous. And close."

Tad kissed the top of her head. "Things have seemed like that since last night at this time."

She smiled. "Let's get some equipment. It's in the cottage. For our journey downriver."

"We're going downriver? Among the water moccasin snakes?"

"They won't bother us. It is not the one-leggeds, but the two-leggeds I am worried about."

"You've got a point."

The cottage was built like a big doll house—all fanciful gingerbread decoration on the outside, one big meeting room on the inside. Linda peeked in a lacy curtained window to see save wildlife posters tacked to cork walls. When she selected a small key from the chain attached to her jeans and placed it into the door's lock, Tad gave out a small whistle.

"Walk With Wildlife gave you a key?"

She looked back over her shoulder. "I have not always been a wanted dead or alive tree hugger, you know."

Tad grinned. "Still, I'd hate to see breaking and entering attached to your offenses."

Linda opened the door and switched on the overhead lights. She walked to a storage area of the room and foraged through drawers until she located two flashlights, insect repellant and a couple of energy bars.

Tad accepted what she provided. "This is great. Let's stay the season. Become swamp things."

"You know, that almost sounds appealing."

Linda then found a key placed under the shelf paper of a middle cutlery drawer. She used it to open a high, locked, compartment. From there she pulled another key and two sheathed hunting knives.

Tad let out a low whistle. "You have high security clearance."

"Before I became a jewel thief."

She handed Tad a knife. "They will fit in our jacket pockets, I think."

"Good."

Linda smiled. They needed so few words between them. She flung the pack over her shoulder. "Let's unlock a canoe."

His brows knit.

She sought to reassure him. "From what our taxi driver said, it sounds like Walk With Wildlife is in trouble with the Garmons, yes?

179

So we're borrowing one of their canoes in a good cause."

"Was Garmon Chemicals a reluctant supporter?"

"At first. And Richard Wunder's actions did not help."

Linda illuminated their path toward the river's edge. Tad followed. "And Neil Garmon was a bigger supporter than the new Lady Garmon, right?"

"Tad, what if Lord Garmon's crackdown on Walk With Wildlife is more than coming over to his wife's way of thinking? What if he is covering for his son? Chief Hawes said Neil has debts. Maybe Lord Garmon thinks Neil might have stolen the necklace and is covering up for him."

"That's possible," Tad agreed.

The sound of the river's rushing flow became louder. "Might our mysterious red-haired woman be meeting Neil Garmon tonight?"

"If she's not another member of the Garmon family herself."

"Or maybe she has an appointment with General Tenatu or his entourage."

"Hmmm. We have been closer to that crowd than is diplomatically advisable lately."

Linda's light fanned out along the trail. A salamander scurried by. The trail widened and she took Tad's hand.

"I am more worried about Wunder and his band of paint throwers."

"Let's not forget Paul Ferris. And Professor Adair. If the woman herself isn't Maille Adair."

"Or Paul Ferris," she reminded him.

Tad laughed. "What a web!"

"*Asiyu.* Grandmother Spider would be proud."

"Well. I'm just confused."

Linda flashed her light on two chained and padlocked canoes nestled in the tall grass beside the river. She pulled the key from her pocket.

"I don't think our confusion will last much longer," she said.

Chapter 22

Linda knelt ahead of him in the eleven-foot fiberglas canoe. She was doing most of the work with her strong, even strokes, although the flow of the river helped.

Tad hadn't known how accomplished she was on the water. He wanted to compliment her on her skill, but once they'd donned the yellow life vests and she'd given him clear instructions on how to enter and leave the bow, how to paddle and steer, they'd established a silent vigilance. Tad felt Linda's confidence in him ease his own misgivings about keeping the canoe level.

They approached the area of Garmon headquarters. Tad could see the lights.

Linda turned only enough for Tad to see her strong profile in the moon's light. "J-stroke. Left," she whispered.

Tad remembered her description of a J-stroke. He pushed his paddle sideways at the end of each movement. He might have been following one of her ancestors 'guidance three hundred years ago, at this very spot, he realized. An ancestor who had a similar, beautiful profile.

"*Waden unega,*" Linda spoke her thanks softly, teasing him with the Cherokee name of white man. He loved her quiet tone and humor. Tad hoped that other *unega* from a long-ago time had been wise enough to follow his guide.

"We should beach it now, I think." It was her first full sentence since they'd been on the river, spoken as quietly as the wind through the pines.

She stopped the canoe by pushing her paddle forward in the water, then brought it skillfully to the riverside.

Linda did most of the work pulling the craft out of the water too. Her first act on shore was to check his bandage-wrapped ribs, worry in her dark eyes.

"I'm all right," Tad whispered. Too loud. His voice carried over the water as hers did not.

She touched his face. "No, not all right. You are too light."

Before he could ask what she meant, she was smearing his face and hair with creek bed mud. Of course. He was not very well camouflaged. He helped smearing the red Georgia clay mud along his hands.

She smiled. "*Asiyu*," she approved, becoming one with her ancestor in his mind. He nodded, letting both of them know his respect for her prowess.

They hadn't walked far when they saw the dim, solar-powered lights of the wildlife habitat river walkway. Beyond them, the Garmon headquarters building loomed, reminding Tad, not of a Frank Lloyd Wright creation, but more of a great crouched bear.

183

He saw the boardwalk reaching out over the river, and its gazebo, where all their troubles began. He felt Linda shiver beside him. The temperature was dropping, but he knew her shiver was from more than a chill.

The area around both banks had been heavily trampled by the emergency workers and investigating police. No one seemed posted around the grounds tonight, although there was plenty of illumination coming from inside the headquarters.

Linda nodded toward a small door surrounded by kudzu vines. Tad squeezed her hand. Yes. That was the door that made a waterway escape possible for the thief of the Connor Emerald. It was black and seemed a fathomless hole, dense in the moonlight. Linda switched on her flashlight.

"What are you—"

"Tracks," she whispered, "from the door. Fresh. Small. High heels. And another pair, heavier. Following."

"Going?"

"To the water."

They followed, taking a parallel path to the riverbank, among the pines. As the sound of the water grew louder, Linda guided her light along the banks in the bend of the river. The mud bore the imprint of a boat—one larger than their canoe.

"Police boat?" Tad whispered.

"They are usually powered. This one came up out of the water, see?"

"I wonder if—" he began, but Linda's fingers closed over his lips. He held his breath, listening.

Choppy, muffled cries filtered up from the tumbling water's sound.

Linda's cedar scent intensified. "Around the bend," she whispered, "Answers."

Tad moved behind her through the undergrowth. He felt the strength draining, even as the fretful crying intensified. Linda stopped, turned. He was breathing hard. He couldn't hide it from her. She opened his jacket, pressed her cool hand into his aching side.

"How have you learned such stealth in the woods, city boy?" she whispered.

Her words gave him renewed energy. "From you, Ahyoka."

They took each other's hand as they neared the rock outgrowth over the bend in the river.

The figure sat on the rock, back to them, shoulders shaking. A fist appeared, hovering over the flowing water. In it, shining amid its glittering diamond setting, was the Connor Emerald.

Chapter 23

The red-haired woman called out over the water. "I followed your instructions! Where are you?"

Linda watched as Lady Garmon's necklace swayed in the woman's grip over the swirling waters of the Chattahoochee. She knew the voice.

And she knew the one who answered it.

"Were you expecting a ghost? That's not my style, darling."

Dr. Milton stepped out from behind a rhododendron bush. He was dressed to match the woman—in a suit that would not have looked out of place in the 1950s. They were a dance couple, from his narrow lapel jacket to her flared skirt. Linda felt Tad's fingers take hers as her teacher approached the woman. "You look wretched. Wipe your eyes. You were a very bad girl. But you followed my instructions, and showed me you can change."

The woman on the rock sat up higher.

"Kent? Is it really you?"

"Of course it's me."

"You're alive."

"Do you think this river can give a physical specimen like me more than a few bumps and bruises?"

186

He sounded too quiet, too calm, like a ghost of himself, Linda thought. The woman flinched when he took hold of her black hair band and removed the wig. Blond hair tumbled out.

Alice, Lady Garmon.

"I'm so sorry Kent. I was angry when I saw you with the girl."

"You were perfect. All part of the plan."

"Plan?"

"I knew you couldn't pull off the theft of your little bauble alone. So I kept up the mystery of who we were going to accuse. But that wouldn't be enough. I had to drive you to an emotional extreme to make you truly distraught, so you could appear the perfect victim."

"That's why you...and the Indian girl? To make me push you off the dock?"

"Exactly. I knew if I stood in the proper spot, I could goad you into it. I practiced that fall from that spot, all summer."

"It was most cruel of you."

"Oh, spare me the fake upper-class intonations! That got old when the tabloids dug up your shopworn Manchester past. Your husband was finding out, too, wasn't he? About how much he'd been deceived? And the son was working on a way back into the old man's confidence. That was hampering your position. Don't con a con man. Let's face it, Alice. I was your last chance to profit before your lord started pulling out the pre-nuptial agreement."

"Was, darling?" Her demeanor changed from woman scorned to cooing lover as she offered a little girl's pout. "Why don't I join you in the depths? Disappear as skillfully as you have?"

He approached with a slouch in his oversized suit. "Oh, your disappearance will be even better."

She gave a nervous little laugh as her grip closed over the necklace. "Really?"

"Really."

"Tad," Linda whispered. "He is going to kill her."

Tad already had the knife out of his pocket. He pulled it from its sheath. Dr. Milton lifted the wig and sent it over the water's flow. "There," he said, watching the river take it downstream. "Bye, bye, Miss American Pie number eighty-seven."

"What?"

"Oh, the first student who sold herself to me for a passing grade? Had her in my old Chevy while that song Miss American Pie was playing. I was a graduate student teacher, she was divorced with two kids who needed my course for her teaching degree. We both got what we wanted, didn't we? Things were so much simpler then.

"Now I like the younger ones. And they need sex education, don't they? But sometimes I have to point out that I hold all the cards—the grade, the transcript recommendation. A few even turn me down! Well, I couldn't have that."

He laughed, covering the sound of Tad's teeth grinding.

"I hear some have gone public against me now," Dr. Milton continued. "So this early demise was a good idea, wasn't it, eighty-seven?" You came with higher stakes. It was a good time, but you lost, Alice."

"Kent! After all I went through for us?"

"Foolish of you, wasn't it? But I imagine you've played many men. Maybe we're two of a kind that way. It was bound to catch up with you. And now you pay."

He stepped on Alice Garmon's wrist, stopping her retreat. Trapping the necklace.

"Now be a good girl," he admonished. "Let go. "I'll make it painless if you let go."

The woman below him screamed.

"Stay," Tad advised Linda. "Back me up?"

She nodded.

"Stand away from her, Dr. Milton," Tad said evenly, standing.

He turned, looked Tad over, his eyes laughing until he saw the knife. But the smile remained.

"Well, Linda's jock. What brings you here? Come to get your baby out of jail?"

"Something like that. And I'm sure the police will be glad they can stop dredging the river for you, sir."

"Oh, they won't stop. Maybe they'll find you right away, so your parents won't have to look at a bloated corpse. They can remember you as their handsome, dim-witted boy. Coming out here was more stupid than tangling with General Tenatu's bodyguards, kid."

Linda watched Lady Garmon transfer the necklace to her free left hand. "Here!" she called before she threw it. A short throw. But Linda wasn't worried. Tad was a wonderful ball player. He lunged forward and caught it on the fly with his left hand. Dr. Milton kicked Lady Garmon as she pulled out of his hold and tried to run. She fell. Her head hit stone with a sickening thud.

Chapter 24

She lay very still. Dr. Milton rammed his foot into her side. "One small push," he told Tad. "That's all it will take to send her into the river. Give me the necklace."

"Move away from her," Tad demanded. Linda saw the gleam of the knife in his right hand flicker. Dr. Milton saw it too. He stepped sideways.

"You don't know how to use that," he said.

He pushed Alice Garmon closer to the rock's edge. Her shoulder and one arm dangled over the water. Dr. Milton grabbed a pistol from the deep pocket of his suit.

"Now be a good boy and drop the knife. I can kill you faster."

Tad shrugged. "You'll kill me anyway. I might as well hold onto both."

"If that's the way you—"

"You cannot kill us both," Linda told him. "And I am very good with a knife."

Dr. Milton looked surprised, but the smile did not leave his face.

"Ah, the lovely Linda. What a team you two are—the brains to your boyfriend's brawn. Yes, you do look at home with your more primitive technology, little Cherokee."

"Your words do not have power to hurt us."

"Oh? Why not?"

"You have not proved worthy of any power."

Tad looped the necklace through his thumb, and took Lady Garmon's pale white arm, dragging her toward him.

Dr. Milton's smiled disappeared as he pointed the gun at Tad's head. "Tell him to stop!"

"Tad. Please," Linda said quietly.

Tad released Lady Garmon's arm.

"Now drop the knife."

Linda nodded.

Tad obeyed and the gun's muzzle came down from its lethal target. It now hovered between Tad and Linda.

"My little fires kept you guessing, didn't they?"

"You set fire to Professor Adair's rooms? Why?"

"She was ungrateful. I thought she wanted to start up our thing again. All she wanted was a look at that damned stone. Well, I enjoyed implicating her, and burning your little good luck dolls as you put out my fires."

Lady Garmon moaned, there at Tad's feet. It distracted Dr. Milton. In that moment Linda took her chance. The knife flew as he turned back to her.

It hit its mark, his wrist, before he fired. Linda dropped to the ground. From there she saw the smoking gun make a wide arc, then land in the waters of the Chatahoochee.

With a look of rage on his face, Dr. Milton went for her. He reached Tad instead, who was holding up the one thing Dr. Milton wanted more than hurting them. Protect yourself, Linda's thought flew. Do not give him such a wide target. But her voice could only scream as Dr. Milton buried his fist into Tad's damaged side.

Tad collapsed under the blow. Linda prayed for speed as she scrambled to her feet.

Dr. Milton grabbled the dangling necklace with a primal yell. He pushed Tad over the rock's edge. The necklace broke, leaving Dr. Milton with a short strand of diamonds as Tad fell into the river with the rest.

The flowing water swallowed Tad and the Connor Emerald.

Linda looked down the rocky embankment. She saw the palm of his hand emerge. So white. She had not smeared that part of him with mud.

She took a deep breath, jumped.

She was caught in mid-air as a pair of impossibly strong arms locked around her. When she struggled, a deep voice sounded at her ear. "Easy," it said.

The arms turned her and she faced two more of the men who had pursued them all day. One had Dr. Milton in a choke hold that held him fast. The other bowed politely.

"Tad?" she cried.

The man who held her walked three long steps. Out of the shadows General Tenatu appeared, dressed in army camouflage and a green cape. He bowed almost as deeply as the soldier had.

"Miss Tassel. Please give my guard Dey-Grebo the honor of retrieving your friend. He is a very fine swimmer."

He nodded in the direction of the riverbank where another bodyguard already had Tad wedged under his arm.

Her guard placed her back on her feet. Linda finally felt herself breathe. She ran for the riverbank.

When Dey-Grebo placed Tad on the grass, she sank to her knees beside him. His tumbling in the Chatahoochee had washed off his mud. She put his head into her lap. General Tenatu placed his own cape over Tad's drenched, shaking form.

His breathing was short and shallow. "Linda."

"Yes."

"You're not hurt?"

"No. Academics are very poor shots. General Tenatu and his bodyguards are here, Tad, see?"

The one who had pulled him from the river took a gold half-moon amulet on a chain from his own neck and placed it around Tad's with a stream of soft words.

The general nodded. "I do not put it into English words well," he said. "But Dey-

Grebo is very sorry for the punch that caused your injury. He was told Miss Tassel, our honored guest, was abducted. By you. Told by that woman." He indicated Lady Garmon, who was pushing away the ministering hands of another bodyguard. "I extend my apologies as well," the general continued. "We wish you peace, good health, and, with your fine warrior woman, heirs to the thousandth generation."

Tad nodded.

"He understands," she told the hovering Liberians. They took a step back as Linda returned her anxious gaze to Tad's face.

"Your lips are blue."

"Just...c-cold."

"Your lungs?"

He breathed a deep, shuddering breath. In. Out. "Working...yes?"

"Yes, fine. But, how? I saw Dr. Milton's hit."

"I heard you. Tell me. To dodge out of the way. Of that punch."

She cleared the wet curls from his forehead. "But I did not say anything."

"Not in words. Your look was scary enough."

Chapter 25

Tad slept as soundly as he could remember, coming out of the dense blackness with dreams of his house filling up with tip-toeing people. The last of them was Linda, throwing her books down on the dining room table as if she lived there. He liked the sound of that.

She put her head in his open bedroom doorway. "Good sleep?"

"Great sleep."

"Ready for company?"

"If it's yours."

She walked in. Tad smiled when she ignored the chair and climbed onto his bed, sitting cross-legged. "There are offerings in the kitchen."

"Like what?"

"Baked goods—oatmeal cookies and custards from your neighbors, my grandmother Longknife's chestnut bread, sent by express mail. You know, comfort food. To help keep you in this bed."

"You would be enough."

"Tad Gist!" She batted her eyelashes dramatically. "You are feeling better!"

He felt his face flaring red. "I didn't mean. I mean, I like you here, and all to myself. Smelling so good. You know."

"Yes," she assured him, coming closer, kissing his cheek. Her hand lingered at his shoulder. "I went to all your professors to collect next week's assignments."

Now he frowned. "You're too kind."

"I know. But before food or assignments, I am to supervise your visitors. Five minutes each, then they must go. Dr. Fine's orders."

"Who all is out there?"

Maille Adair put her head in through the doorway. "Nice dragons," she complimented Maggie's gallery of protection taped up around his bed.

Tad grinned. "Professor Adair, come in! Glad to see you haven't disappeared."

"And I understand I have you two to thank that the rest of my apartment didn't disappear."

"We're sorry about your bedroom."

"It could have been a lot worse. And put my neighbors in danger, too. Listen, I'm reinstated at Morris now that my IRA terrorist connections appear to have been manufactured out of whole cloth by Dr. Milton and his not-so-ladylike Lady Garmon." I received apologies and, after this semester, a six-month sabbatical to finish my thesis, which of course was well backed up. My melted computer did not erase it from the earth."

"That's great."

"And the Chatahoochee got the emerald."

"They haven't found it?"

"No. And they may not, ever. It's that kind of river, remember?"

"That's...good?"

"Of course! The Connor Emerald is out of English hands at last! It is being held securely by a river in a country where more people of Irish blood live than Ireland itself! Being held, perhaps, to rise again when it's needed? Oh, this is going to be a thesis that would make the warrior poets of Erie proud!"

She dropped papers and her foil-wrapped offering in Linda's lap.

"Here are your assignments for my class and some Irish soda bread. Homemade. With raisins. *Dia liomsha,* you two."

Their re-instated teacher headed out the door.

"I think we've just been wished deep blessings," Tad informed Linda. "Mom sent me to the Irish Cultural center heritage programs long enough to translate that."

Next came W. C. Hawes, carrying a trout packed in ice for his offering. "Were you really going to arrest Linda?" Tad asked their friend.

"I had a warrant. But just between you and me and the lamp post, I'd neglected to have it signed. Getting forgetful in my old age."

"Who caused the warrant? Who testified against Linda?"

"A federal bright light who was trying to avoid an international incident. This sterling fellow thought one of General Tenatu's bodyguards saw Linda send Milton over the railing. But through our multiple translators we finally realized he saw a woman who fit the description of Lady Garmon much better. And what he witnessed took place before the lights went out, not after. What a merry chase you two gave Dey-Grebo and his apology gifts!"

"There were plenty of misunderstandings to go around, sir."

"Listen, next time you two play detective, do it north of the Mason Dixon line, will you? I would like to go back to my peaceful semi-retirement, and I'm clean out of favors to pull out of my old haunts."

When Paul Ferris visited his room next, he'd earned Kelsey Doyle's arm around his shoulders. Tad's mom had found another stray, he figured. And this one could cook. "Five courses, Tad!" she proclaimed happily. "Wait until you can sit at the table with us again, with Paul as our guest."

"Always your honored servant, Madame," Paul corrected her, handing over a cup of gumbo. "First course for tonight. Enjoy."

When they were all gone, Linda and Tad shared the best soup they'd ever had. Then she began collecting their offerings. "Social hour is over," she said.

"I'm not tired. I slept all afternoon."

She looked in their empty soup cup. "Still hungry?"

"Always."

She climbed up on the bed and stretched out beside him. He eased her closer and felt her sigh. They would always fit together like this, he was sure.

"Gus Mitchel sent over a pint of chocolate chip. Shall we skip to dessert?"

He grinned. "Sure."

The End

Readers we need you.

Please leave a review, even a one liner counts, and has a big influence on our future sales.

2022 Bestselling Author
Eileen Charbonneau

Eileen Charbonneau's stories explore the perspectives of people often left out of history: women, first peoples, immigrants, and the marginalized in her fiction for adults and young readers. She lives in the brave little state of Vermont with her husband. She adores him, their kids and grandchild. Eileen loves reading, attending good plays and movies, exploring her state, country and world. Oh, and Vermont maple creemies. (write to her at eileencharbonneau@gmail.com and she'll tell you what they are!)

You can find her at:
https://bookswelove.net/charbonneau-eileen/
www.eileencharbonneau.com
email: eileencharbonneau@gmail.com
twitter: @EileenC1988
Facebook: Eileen Charbonneau Author
Instagram: eileencharbonneau
Blogs
http://manituwak.blogspot.com
https://bwlauthors.blogspot.com

BWL Publishing

bwlpublishing.ca